ALL YOU NEED IS LOVE

A WALKER BEACH ROMANCE

LINDSAY HARREL

For my husband and sons:
You are my biggest dream come true.

CHAPTER 1

*N*ormally, life in the slow lane suited Shannon Baker just fine.

But three months or more to become a foster mom—to become Noah's mom?

That was an eternity.

The water lapped at her bare feet as she walked the wet shoreline, flip-flops dangling from her fingers. As she'd expect at eleven o'clock on a Saturday, the beach was already crowded with locals and tourists alike, but Shannon only had attention for the boy she hoped one day to adopt.

Several feet ahead, Noah Robinson tossed a football to Lucky and laughed as the golden retriever took off into the fringes of the California surf. Shannon closed her eyes for a moment, relishing the five-year-old's giggles pealing across the same breeze that lifted Shannon's hair off her shoulders.

Noah's joy, the late-June sun on Shannon's face, the crisp scent of coconut sunscreen and brine—it all soothed the parts of her soul left ruffled by her call from the foster care agency yesterday to confirm the processing of her application.

She had hoped that her role as a preschool teacher might

speed along the process of bringing Noah into her home. But the agency worker had been clear that it would take just as long for her as any other applicant.

Which meant, in the meantime, Noah faced even more uncertainty. And his short life had already been filled with so much.

When combined with the thought that tonight she'd have to face her sister Quinn for the first time in forever—*thank you, Baker family reunion*—it was almost enough for Shannon to bury herself in a heap of blankets and stay curled up all day watching Hallmark Christmas movies in the middle of summer.

But here she was, fighting the urge to turn inward. Fighting to keep the peace in her own heart. Fighting for Noah's sake.

The blond-haired boy raced after Lucky toward the north end of the beach, where rocks curved into a magnificent cove that divided the beach from a six-acre community park on the other side.

"Noah!" Shannon cupped her hands around her mouth. "Don't go too far."

"Okay!" But as soon as he reached the rocks, he disappeared from sight.

There wasn't anywhere for him to go past the rocky cove, and he could swim, but that didn't stop Shannon from chasing after him, her heart banging against her ribs until she caught sight of the boy hugging Lucky at the edge of the water. For the first time since she'd picked him up from his current foster home this morning, he'd stopped moving, staring out across the ocean.

He'd grown so much in the two years since she'd met him. A recent spurt had left his bathing suit two inches higher than his knees, but in this moment, he was the same three-year-old she'd had to comfort when his grandma Mary had dropped him off in Shannon's classroom for the first time.

The faraway gaze in his precious blue eyes, the way he bit his bottom lip so it didn't tremble, his arms wrapped tight around Lucky's neck—they all socked Shannon in the gut, a reminder that he was lost. No matter how brave and confident and friendly he'd grown since that first day of school, a boy simply didn't get over his mother leaving him behind to chase other dreams.

And with his former-neighbor-turned-foster-mom moving out of state by the end of the summer, he needed someone he could count on. She wanted to be that person.

Shannon dropped her shoes on the ground, squatted beside Noah, and placed her hand on his back. "You okay, bud?"

He glanced at her, his freckled nose scrunched. "Miss Florence is taking me to see Grandma tomorrow."

"Is she?" His foster mom hadn't mentioned it when Shannon had picked him up this morning. "That will be nice."

Noah plopped onto the ground and leaned toward her, his soft curls tickling her neck as she slid her arm around him. "What if her memory is so bad that she doesn't know who I am?"

Oh, bud. How she wished she could assure him that would never happen. But with Mary Robinson's recent diagnosis of Alzheimer's, it was almost inevitable at some point. Shannon squeezed the boy and kissed the top of his head. "Even if your grandma's mind can't always remember, her heart will never forget you. How could anyone forget such a wonderful boy?"

Noah snuggled closer as the water lapped in and out.

Rocks skittered behind them, and a low growl rumbled in Lucky's throat, breaking the peace of the moment. The dog bounded toward the rocks and barked a few sharp warnings.

"Lucky!" Shannon's arm dropped from Noah's shoulders and she pivoted from her spot on the ground. "Wha—"

The question caught in her throat at the sight of a man standing not ten feet away, his hands held up as if a police officer had ordered him to surrender. "Whoa, boy."

Shannon scrambled to her feet. She should call Lucky off, but her tongue stuck to the roof of her mouth.

The man cleared his throat. "I'm sorry to interrupt, but—"

Lucky advanced a step, another deep growl breaking the man's speech. The guy took a step back.

Shannon shook herself from her stupor. "Lucky. Heel."

Her dog whipped his head around, big brown eyes mournful, but he eventually trotted to her side.

I'm so sorry. Why wouldn't the words come out of her mouth? Sure, she didn't have an affinity for chatting up strangers like her cousin Ashley, and she wasn't a take-charge type like her soon-to-be cousin Bella, but she *did* have common decency.

And yet, when a well-dressed man with gel-tousled brown hair, deep chocolate eyes, olive skin, and a straight Grecian nose looked at her, apparently Shannon's manners disappeared. All she could do was stand there like an idiot, blinking hard as if sand had settled into her eyelids. If only she had that excuse.

"Hi." Noah's voice sliced through the silence, causing Shannon to jump. Before she could remind Noah not to talk to strangers, the boy moved around her and toward the man. "My name's Noah."

"Hey, Noah. I'm Marshall." The guy's face lit up with a grin—and goodness, his five-o'clock scruff made it hard to tell, but were those dimples on either side of his mouth?

Didn't matter that it was only seventy-something degrees out and Shannon wore shorts and a tank top. She was sweating. "Noah, let's not bother the poor man."

The boy's shoulders drooped at her words. He dragged his feet back toward the ocean, pulling Lucky along with him.

"He wasn't bothering me. I'm afraid I was unintentionally bothering you." Marshall stuck his hands into the pockets of his khaki shorts as he came to stand beside her. He wore a white button-up shirt rolled to his elbows, and his silver watch winked in the sunlight. Hints of some sort of exotic cologne filled the air between them.

He definitely was *not* from Walker Beach. She'd have remembered him for sure.

"You just surprised us. I didn't hear you coming at all." Shannon toed the sand before forcing herself to glance up into his eyes.

Her efforts were rewarded with another view of his dimples —yep, they were definitely there. "That's because I was here the whole time." He nodded at the rocks. "I got into town way too late to explore last night, so this morning I found myself wandering the beach and ended up in this little cove."

"And then we broke your peaceful retreat. I'm so sorry. And sorry about my dog. He doesn't act like that unless I'm being threatened." She winced. "Not that you were threatening us. He just misread the situation." Goodness, she was rambling.

But she didn't usually talk to guys she didn't know extremely well. Shannon Baker had never been *that* girl—bold, smooth, flirtatious. Not like Quinn.

Thankfully, Marshall ignored her blathering and offered an easy laugh. "No worries. That's the best kind of dog." He looked at Noah and Lucky, who were knee-high splashing in the waves together. "He's really good with your son."

"Oh, he's n—" Shannon hesitated. "He's not my son ... yet."

"Yet?"

"I'm hoping to adopt him."

Her chest warmed at the thought of Noah moving into Bella's old room. In anticipation of her wedding next weekend, her former roommate had already moved into the house she and Shannon's cousin Ben were renting just a few miles away. Afterward, Shannon had made a whirlwind trip to Herman Hardware and purchased paint and a few decorations to get the room ready for Noah.

While she'd painted, she'd dreamed of their future. Of

stargazing on summer nights and curling up by the fireplace reading stories during the winter. Of learning about sports for the first time because Noah was interested in baseball. Of giving the boy a sense of security he could count on for as long as she had the ability to provide it.

Shannon may not be a former NFL player like her brother, a business owner and town leader like her parents, or a hotshot marketing executive like her sister, but she *could* do this one meaningful thing with her life.

A tear slid down her cheek. She swiped it away.

"You all right?"

Oh. Right. Marshall was still here. What was she thinking, being so vulnerable in front of a stranger? "Y-yes. Sorry."

"Hey, don't apologize. I find your honesty refreshing."

Her eyes shot toward his again, but no, his serious gaze seemed just as genuine as his tone. Still ... "We should leave you in peace."

"Eh, peace is overrated."

It was totally her imagination, but the way he looked at her —gaze narrowed but soft—made her feel like he saw something there worth knowing. But that was ridiculous. She wasn't anything special.

Besides, she'd misread a guy's interest before, and she wasn't making that mistake again. "I have a dinner to get ready for, and ..." Her excuse trailed off.

"Ah, I see." A tease lit his eyes. "Hot date with your boyfriend?"

Sudden laughter burst from her throat. "Um, no." What would this guy say if he knew Shannon had never been on a date, much less had a boyfriend?

In the distance, seagulls swooped into the water, hunting for a late breakfast.

She pointed at Noah. "Besides my dad, brother, and a passel of cousins and uncles, *that* is the only man in my life."

As if sensing Shannon's attention, the kid looked up and waved with a smile. Shannon smiled back. Yes, they were going to be okay, despite it taking longer than she'd like to get approved as a foster mom.

Once Florence moved, even if the foster care approval process was still ongoing, Shannon could petition for Noah to be placed with her on an emergency basis so he could stay with someone he knew and trusted. But getting that placement wasn't a given. Of course, she'd already connected with Noah's social worker Miranda Shubert on several occasions. Now, she just had to wait for the foster care agency—which was located one town over—to schedule her interview and get the ball officially rolling.

Basically, the whole thing was a hurry-up-and-wait situation.

Marshall squinted at Noah. "I mean, he's a little short, but I can see his appeal."

Shannon couldn't help but giggle. Oy, she must sound like a schoolgirl to this sophisticated guy, not a twenty-seven-year-old woman.

Marshall studied her for a beat before looking away and clearing his throat. "Hey, do you mind if I play a round of catch with Noah before you go?"

Really? He wasn't anxious to escape? "No, I don't mind."

"Great." He jogged toward Noah, holding up a hand and shouting something the wind carried away.

Moving back toward the rock where apparently Marshall had sat not twenty minutes ago, Shannon hunkered down to watch as Marshall and Noah tossed the football back and forth along the stretch of beach tucked away from the rest of the town. Lucky bounded between them, following the trajectory of the ball in an attempt to retrieve it.

A strange sensation slowly worked its way through Shannon's veins as she looked on. Something about the scene in front of her called, beckoned—demanded she stop sitting on the sidelines. Standing, Shannon brushed off the sand clinging to the backs of her legs and walked toward the guys.

Noah cheered as she approached Marshall. He lobbed the ball her way and she grimaced, squeezing her eyes shut as she held out her hands in an attempt to catch it. It gave a telltale *thwack* as it hit the ground.

"You know, it's a lot easier to catch when you can actually see it coming." Marshall leaned down to pick up the ball and slipped it into her fingers.

"You'd think I'd know that by now. My brother used to play football." She turned and lobbed the ball toward Noah—or attempted to, anyway. It fell pathetically short, giving Lucky the chance he'd been looking for to swoop in and steal it. He took off running toward the rocks, Noah shouting and hot on his trail. "Well, it's official. I'm going to be the worst boy mom ever."

"No way. I don't even know your name and I can tell you're going to be an amazing mother."

His declaration stole her breath.

It was dumb to be so affected by the confidence in a total stranger's tone, but still it meant something to her. Not even her parents had seemed so sure of her decision to adopt when she'd informed them about it a little over a week ago.

She hugged her waist. "Shannon." The word came out a whisper.

Marshall cocked his head, moved closer. "What?"

She tilted her chin upward—he had to be nearing six feet tall to her five-five—licked her lips, and tried again. "My name is Shannon."

"That's a beautiful name for a beautiful woman."

She blinked, stepped back, shook herself from the trance. Because guys just didn't say things like that.

Well, they said them to her sister Quinn all the time.

But not to Shannon.

8

Clearly he was just an outrageous flirt.

His eyebrows scrunched together and he massaged the back of his neck. "Sorry, I really never say things like that. But today, I'm ... not quite myself."

Oh.

Before Shannon could respond, Noah bounded back over, huffing, while a dejected Lucky followed. "Miss Shannon, can we try throwing again?"

"Of course, bud. I'll try to do better this time."

They spread out once more, forming a triangle. But it didn't matter how much she wanted to catch the ball—it slipped through her fingers every time. No wonder she'd nearly failed PE in high school.

Marshall jogged over. "I don't want to interfere, but would you like some pointers?"

"Yes, please."

And for the next fifteen minutes, he showed her the best way to position her hands to catch a ball above her waist and below it. She mixed them up several times, but then, miracle of miracles, she caught one.

Squealing, she held it up in triumph, and both Marshall and Noah ran toward her, whooping and celebrating with her. Noah threw his arms around her waist, and she caught Marshall's eye over his head. She mouthed *Thank you*, and he grinned in reply.

As soon as Noah let go, turning to run through the waves with Lucky once more, Marshall approached, holding up his hand for a high five. "Nice work."

"Thanks." She slapped his palm, and his fingers curled around hers for a moment longer than necessary.

A lump caught in her throat at the feel of her small hand in his larger one. When he dropped it, the tingle of his touch remained.

"I couldn't have done it without my awesome coach." Her lips tipped into a grin that grew serious far too quickly. "But really, thank you. You sure made a little boy's day. He hasn't had too many great ones lately and …" She sucked a breath between her teeth. Sudden exhaustion overtook her bones, and, frowning, Shannon sat down.

Marshall joined her, his strong forearms wrapped around his knees. "He's a great kid. And he obviously is enamored with you."

She ran her finger through the sand, at first drawing simple lines, then arcing out into a small picture. A house. A sun. "He doesn't know any better." Her attempt at a joke fell flat, as evidenced by Marshall's silence. Clearing her throat, she continued with the design.

"If you don't mind me asking, how do you know him?"

"I was his preschool teacher for two years. His grandma has had custody of him for a little longer than that, ever since his mom left to pursue an acting career in Los Angeles."

And then, as if she'd known this man forever, Shannon told him about her relationship with Noah, about Mary's mental decline, about how the final straw was her leaving Noah at the mall six weeks ago because she'd forgotten he was with her. "Social services removed him from the home, and Mary moved into a memory care facility. He's been with his neighbor ever since, but she and her family are moving out of state soon."

"So you're going to adopt him?"

"That's the plan. I was hoping I could get foster certification fast-tracked since I already have fingerprint clearance and a background check due to my job. But there's just so much left in the process—an interview, adoption and fostering classes, psychiatric evaluation, home inspection—and each step takes time." Shannon added a woman to her sand picture. "So for a while, he'll have to live with someone else."

Marshall turned his face toward her, using his hand to block the sun that had slowly moved a bit farther westward. Whoa. It must be about two in the afternoon. How had three hours gone by so quickly? "Don't get me wrong, I think it's awesome. I'm just wondering why *you're* the one adopting him."

"If not me, then who?" She shrugged. "His social worker hasn't been able to get ahold of his mom, and he doesn't have any other family willing to take him. Walker Beach is an amazing community, but it's small. I'm afraid he'd eventually be sent to a town with more foster home options. But he should be able to stay near his grandma, the only family he has."

Shannon finished off her picture with a little boy holding hands with the woman. "Besides, I can't help but love him. And really, all you need is love to make a thing work, right?" Love—and a good dose of humility.

"Hmm." A pause. "Hey, you're an artist."

She glanced up to find his eyes studying her silly picture. "Oh, that's ... no. It's nothing."

"It's not nothing." He leaned in just a touch. "And neither are you."

If Shannon were made of ice, she'd be a puddle on the ground by now.

Sheesh. She needed to get control of her seesawing emotions. This was so silly. Marshall didn't know her. She didn't know him.

So how had his words stroked a hurting place in her heart that few even knew existed?

Shannon dusted off her hands and stood. "I had a really nice time with you, but I need to get Noah home."

Marshall pushed himself off the ground, then checked his watch. "Wow, it's later than I thought. I'd better get going as well."

They both stood there for a moment, looking at each other, the moment holding, suspended in time.

What was happening? Surely she was imagining this connection between them.

Shannon pulled her gaze from his. "Noah! Lucky! Time to go."

"Aw, man!" But despite his protest, the boy dragged his feet, hanging onto Lucky's collar as he trudged toward her.

She turned back to Marshall. "Thank you for teaching me to catch. And for listening while I talked your ear off."

There had been something so freeing about sharing with someone she'd never see again. Because in a town the size of this one, everyone knew everyone else's business. And to them, Shannon Baker was merely the "shyest" member of the ginormous Baker clan, the daughter of the local pizza parlor owners, the younger sister of twins Tyler and Quinn.

The one always in her sister's vibrant and terrifying shadow.

But Marshall No Name from Who Knew Where—he only saw what she'd shown him. Whether he recognized it or not, he'd given her a gift. The ability, for a brief moment in time, to be more than she could be otherwise.

"It was my pleasure." He opened his mouth as if to say something, then closed it. Frowned. "Maybe I'll see you around?"

He wasn't going to ask for her number then. But what did she expect? She may have momentarily felt like Cinderella at the ball, but he was obviously someone else's Prince Charming.

Besides, she didn't have time for romance anyway. Her attention needed to stay focused on Noah's adoption. And, more immediately, on the Baker family reunion. She was kind of in charge of the whole thing since her cousin Ashley had handed it over to her last month.

Shannon forced a smile. "Maybe."

"Would it be weird to ask for a hug?" And there was the adorably charming grin he'd flashed at her more than once today—the one that toasted her insides. "I mean, you did kind of tell me your life story."

Biting her lip, she studied him. "And yet I know almost nothing about you."

His features darkened for a moment, then neutralized again with a shrug. "Not much to tell. Although I will say ... I felt more myself today than I have in a really long time. So thank you, Shannon."

Then he stepped forward and, after pausing to give her time to escape if she wanted to—she didn't—enveloped her in a hug. Now she could tell that his cologne smelled like cinnamon and some sort of flowers. Geraniums, maybe? Whatever it was, the combination was heady, as was the all-too-brief sensation of being in his arms.

Even if her proverbial midnight had finally arrived, *this* was what dreams were made of.

As Marshall stepped back, Shannon snagged Noah's hand in hers, whispered goodbye, tucked this perfect day away in her heart, and put on her game face.

Because dinner with her family—including Quinn—was just hours away.

And that was enough to spoil almost any fairytale.

CHAPTER 2

*H*e hadn't thought women like her really existed.

Marshall St. John kept his gaze fixed on Shannon, her long blonde hair swaying against her retreating back. If he were a different kind of man, he'd have asked her out in a heartbeat. But he didn't do serious relationships. And sure, he'd only spent a few hours with Shannon, but he instinctively knew that she was a forever-relationship kind of girl.

His gut twisted at the thought, but he pushed it away. It didn't matter anyway. He lived three thousand miles away in New York City, and he was only here in Walker Beach for one reason—to snag a promotion back home.

He couldn't afford to lose his focus now, not when he was so close. Even if the distraction came with huge blue eyes, a tiny waist, and a heart that, far as he could tell, was more genuine than any Marshall had encountered since his mom was alive.

Checking his watch again, he grimaced and took off at a brisk pace toward his home for the next nine days. The beach was much more crowded than it'd been hours ago when he'd first come this way, wondering not for the first time how he'd gotten himself into this mess. After all, he wasn't exactly the lying type. And yet, his coworker's proposition had been too tempting to pass up.

Besides, the lie wasn't going to hurt anyone. It was only designed to help two people in a business-like arrangement.

Marshall hopped up onto the boardwalk that ran the length of downtown. Bicyclists, in-line skaters, and dog walkers crowded the scenic route, which gave a fantastic view of both the ocean to the west and the mature oak trees and hills extending out just east of Main Street. Even the backsides of the downtown shops along the boardwalk were quaint, their wooden frames painted a cheerful collection of pastels.

It was so completely foreign to the New Yorker in him.

But the kid from Blakestown, Iowa … he remembered well the small-town vibe. The charm. The community.

The gossip that tore lives apart.

Grunting, Marshall swerved around a young mom with a stroller and headed down the alley between two buildings onto Main Street, past the golf course and marina at the south end of town, and into an older residential neighborhood. After passing a few larger homes, he came to the house on Berry Street where he was staying.

Marshall pushed open the red front door and dropped his keys and wallet on the oak entryway table before making his way into the modest-sized living room, where three pairs of eyes swung to meet him. His hosts, Tyler and Gabrielle Baker, sat together on the couch. Tyler's beefy arm was slung behind his wife, whose hands rested on her very pregnant stomach.

And there, on the leather love seat beside the white brick fireplace, sat Quinn. She flicked a counterfeit smile his way. "Honey, you're back."

Marshall tried to hold back a cringe at the endearment—and the biting tone edging his coworker's lilting voice. With her perfectly styled brown curls, delicate features, and an impressive height that almost matched his own, the woman was beautiful, of that there was no doubt. But Marshall had never been attracted to her, and his lack of attraction had nothing to do with the faint scar trailing down the entire right side of her face.

No, he hadn't known Quinn Baker for five minutes before he realized she was just like so many women he'd met in New York—aggressive, hyper-focused, determined to be the center of attention and the maker of her own success. Which, in and of themselves, were not bad qualities, except when accompanied by a certain coldness that lent itself to selfish ambition.

So unlike Shannon, the blonde-haired, small-town girl with a heart of gold.

Wow, he really needed to forget about her. Not like he'd ever see her again, and making up some romantic fantasy in his mind wouldn't help him zero in on his mission objective.

Which, ironically, included pretense of a whole other level.

"Marshall? Where were you, babe?"

He blinked and refocused on Quinn, whose eyebrows were plucked in such a way that she always appeared to be arching them in question. "I was walking along the beach and lost track of time."

Gabrielle pushed a lock of dark blonde hair behind her ear and snuggled back into Tyler's embrace. "It's a charming town, isn't it? New York is beautiful in its own way, but I'm so glad we decided to settle here."

She and her husband both worked full time at Tyler's non-profit, the Amazing Kids Foundation, which was based out of Midtown Manhattan. They'd traveled back and forth for more than half a year, a home in both locations. But when Gabrielle had gotten pregnant a few months after their wedding last fall, they'd decided Walker Beach was a better place to raise a family and had sold Tyler's apartment in New York.

Marshall wouldn't be caught dead living in a small town again, but not everyone had had his experiences. Still, he couldn't deny Walker Beach's charm. "It definitely is beautiful."

Just like a certain blonde …

Focus.

Quinn stood. "I'd love to hear all about your morning, but we need to be getting ready for dinner at Mom and Dad's."

"Calm down, sis. We have like three hours." The easy laugh lines around Tyler's eyes were proof of his status as the more laid-back twin.

"I know it may not take *you* a long time to get ready, but some of us have hair and makeup to do. Right, Gabrielle?" Quinn shot her sister-in-law a secretive smile.

"Oh, well, I'm mostly ready to go." Gabrielle yawned. "Though I wouldn't say no to a nap."

"I've got work I can do in the meantime." Tyler fixed his gaze on Marshall. "Unless you want to grab a soda with me."

Marshall's mouth went dry. He'd known Tyler for a year or two now, ever since his foundation had hired Marshall and Quinn's agency to run marketing and PR campaigns for them. And he'd already shown his surprise last night over finding Marshall accompanying Quinn on this trip. "You're *my sister's mysterious boyfriend? I knew she was dating someone at work, but I didn't even suspect it was you.*"

Thankfully, Quinn had changed the subject, saving Marshall from having to confirm the bald-faced lie, but the guilt still sat in the pit of his stomach, eating away at the lining.

"Um, sure, we could do that."

"Actually"—Quinn slipped her hand inside Marshall's—"I need my man to myself for a bit first."

Before Tyler could respond, she tugged Marshall down the short hallway, past the future nursery where his stuff sat next to an air mattress, and into the guest bedroom where she was staying. Quinn dropped his hand as soon as she shut the door behind them.

"Thanks." Marshall scratched behind his ear and plopped

onto the edge of the queen-sized bed. "I'm a little nervous that your brother might be onto us."

Quinn waved her hand in the air. "You're being paranoid." She squatted down to rummage through her Dolce & Gabbana suitcase on the floor beside the dresser. "He's probably just wondering how he missed the fact we were dating. But it's not like he and I spend that much time together. Plus, he's been a little distracted since last summer when he and Gabrielle got back together."

"Right."

Standing, a new outfit in hand, Quinn moved to the side table and checked her phone, which was plugged into a charger. "Speaking of distracted, where were you really this morning?" She turned and crossed her arms. "You're still committed to this, right? Because if you're going to play my doting boyfriend, you should actually be around me. Otherwise Tyler *is* going to get suspicious."

"Yes, I'm still committed." He pressed his molars together tight. "So long as you are still committed to recommending me for upper management when we get back."

Quinn turned again, tapped the home button on her phone, scrolled for a moment. "Yes, of course."

Something about her voice sounded almost unsure. An anomaly for her. "Quinn?"

She dropped the phone back onto the table and spun on her heel. "What?" Her tone snapped across the room. Then she took in a deep breath before speaking again. "Sorry. This is nerve-racking for me too, you know."

"Then why do it? Surely your family would have understood you showing up alone."

When she'd approached him with the idea yesterday afternoon—one hour after her boyfriend Edward had dumped her and three hours before she had to leave for the airport to fly to her family's reunion—he'd barely had time to think.

But Quinn had known exactly how to get him to agree to her request. Everyone in the office knew he'd been working his tail off for weeks in hopes of securing the open Director of Digital Strategy position, which his coworker Dylan was also vying for. And as the Group Account Director of their boutique firm, Quinn held a huge sway with the company president, Hugh.

The only aspect of the plan that had tripped him up—had almost made him say no immediately—was that he'd have to travel to California.

He made it a point to avoid being in the same state as his father.

But since Walker Beach was hours from Los Angeles, he'd agreed. Still, Marshall had hardly thought through any of Quinn's outrageous plan, just the end result. He'd had only enough time to swing past his apartment, pack his suitcase, and meet her at their gate at JFK, where they'd waited for about ten minutes before the flight loaded. Then he'd been shoved into a middle seat between a rather robust woman and a mom with her newborn, leaving him little chance to talk through the details with Quinn.

Now, though, they finally had a moment to breathe. Maybe she'd open up to him.

But the way she'd set her lips into a frown didn't bode well for that hope. "Look, Marshall, I realize that this feels a bit ... crazy. But all you need to remember is that we've been together for six months, have kept it a secret at work, and that we're in love and very happy. Let me lead the conversation if it turns to questions about our relationship. Do you think you can do that?"

Not for the first time, he wondered how in the world they were supposed to fool anyone. He'd worked with Quinn for five years now and hardly knew anything about her—except her professional reputation. She'd climbed the corporate ladder of their firm quickly, in large part due to her smarts and worka-holic tendencies.

Not unlike him, really.

He sighed, stood. "All right." Then he headed for the door.

"Marshall."

Turning, he quirked an eyebrow at Quinn. "Yeah?"

She studied him for a moment, her skin pale against the black ruffled comforter. "Thank you. This … it means a lot."

"Sure." He left the guest room and went into his, logged onto his computer, and worked for the next few hours answering emails, including one from Bask Inc., a toiletries company he'd been courting for months. If he landed an account with them, it would be a huge coup for his resume. That combined with Quinn's recommendation should secure him the director posi-tion for sure.

Finally, he hopped in the shower and got dressed just in time to hear a knock. "Come in."

Tyler stuck his head through the doorway. "You ready, man? We're going to walk to my parents' now."

"Yep." He followed Tyler into the hallway and toward the front door, where Gabrielle waited in a pair of shorts and a purple tank top that hugged her belly. Quinn appeared from the hallway right after them, dressed in white ankle pants that clung to her curves, a black shirt that easily cost a few hundred, red heels, and makeup done to perfection.

As a group, they walked two blocks toward one of the largest houses on the street. Instead of knocking, Tyler opened the door and called into the house. "Mom, Dad, we're here."

Marshall's palms began to sweat. Quinn looped her arm through his and leaned close. "We've got this."

He barely had time to nod before she pulled him through the door and into a living room with wood floors, white leather couches, white curtains, pale seafoam-green walls, and silver knickknacks on the custom white oak coffee table.

Then a petite woman with silver-blonde hair rounded the corner and held out her arms. "Quinn, baby! You're home."

Quinn stiffened beside Marshall but dropped his arm so she could embrace the woman. "Hey, Mom."

Her mother pulled back, tears glistening in her eyes, and turned her attention to Marshall. "And you must be Quinn's boyfriend."

He held out his hand. "Marshall St. John. A pleasure to meet you, Mrs. Baker."

"Genevieve, please." Then, despite her slight frame, she tugged him into a hug too. "Come on in, you all. Dinner will be ready soon. Dad's grilling steaks out back."

After quick hugs for Tyler and Gabrielle, Genevieve led the way through a brightly lit hallway toward a kitchen that looked like something out of a home decor magazine. His entire Brooklyn apartment could probably fit into this kitchen. Maybe after his promotion, he'd be able to afford something bigger.

Quinn grabbed his hand, gave him a meaningful look, and whooshed him through the sliding screen door onto a raised deck with a gorgeous view of the marina and ocean not a half-mile away. The sharp scent of smoke and peppercorn emanated from the built-in grill, where a thin, balding man stood in a blue apron. At the sight of Quinn, he set his grilling spatula and mitt down, strode over, and hugged his daughter.

When he pulled back, Quinn stepped away and reclaimed Marshall's hand. "Marshall, this is my dad, Thomas Baker. Daddy, this is my boyfriend, Marshall St. John."

Something clattered to the ground behind them, and they all turned to find a petite woman with an overturned plastic bowl of potato salad spilled at her feet.

Marshall sucked in a sharp breath. What was Shannon doing here?

"And that is my clumsy baby sister, Shannon." Quinn's voice

held a smirk, but Marshall didn't turn to see if the expression on her face matched.

He couldn't look away from Shannon, whose high cheekbones were spotted red and set against a pale face otherwise drained of color.

Sister?

"Boyfriend?" Shannon squeaked.

He wanted to step forward, to explain the situation, to assure her that he hadn't lied—not to her. Not that he'd ever said he was single and available, but the way he'd acted, called her beautiful...

"Why do you sound so surprised?" Quinn interlaced their fingers together. "You knew I was bringing him with me."

"Right." Ducking her head, Shannon knelt to turn the bowl right side up.

And Marshall couldn't help it. He strode toward her, squatted, and helped her scoop the chunks of potato, pickles, and hard-boiled egg into the red container. "Shannon..." He whispered her name, begging her to look at him.

But she just grabbed the bowl and raced back into the house.

"I forgot." Quinn snagged a cloth napkin off the glass-topped patio table and handed it to him. "She's super shy around guys."

Guess he could see that. This morning, she'd been adorably awkward with him at first, but eventually she'd opened up. Thanking her, Marshall took the napkin and cleaned off his fingers, which smelled strongly of mustard and mayo.

Shannon was here. *Here.*

This never would have happened in New York. There, the chances of seeing Shannon again would be a million to one. And she definitely wouldn't have turned out to be his fake girlfriend's sister.

Yet another strike against small towns.

It took fifteen more minutes before the steaks were finished. In that time, Tyler grabbed him a beer and Marshall shot the breeze with the men while the women gathered food inside. He tried to concentrate on their questions about his job —thankfully they steered clear of the topic of his and Quinn's "relationship"—but Marshall couldn't help but sneak glances toward the back door, hoping for a peek at Shannon again. The other women made appearances, setting the table and asking the men their drink preferences, but Shannon stayed tucked away inside until everything was ready and everyone else was seated at the table. Finally, she appeared and sat across from Marshall.

From the seat next to him, Quinn snagged his hand once more. Her cold skin pricked his.

Genevieve served him iced tea and Thomas plopped a huge steak on his plate. The family passed salad, fruit, and asparagus —the potato salad conspicuously missing—and chatted about the latest local news. Apparently Quinn's family owned Froggies, a pizza place in town, and they invited him to try it sometime this week in between family reunion festivities.

Then the conversation moved on to Quinn and work. She chatted about her latest accomplishments—the three huge accounts she'd recently landed—and her new apartment overlooking Prospect Park in an up-and-coming neighborhood of Brooklyn. As Marshall bit into his steak, the butter and salt popping on his tongue, he let his eyes wander to Shannon. Her small nose flared just slightly and her tiny chin trembled as she watched Quinn.

Their gazes connected for a split second and Marshall tried out an encouraging smile. But as soon as he did, Shannon's eyes jerked back to her plate and she shoved a bite of carrot into her mouth.

"It sounds as if you are doing well, Quinn." Genevieve's smile was genuine. "Not that I expected any less from my oldest."

"She's only the oldest by three minutes. Come on."

Tyler's good-natured tease had almost everyone chuckling,

even Quinn, who rolled her eyes. "Three minutes is three minutes, baby brother."

"All right, you two, that's enough." Genevieve turned her attention to Shannon. "Your sister has some big news to share with everyone."

Shannon's jaw clenched. "That's okay, Mom. Tonight isn't about me. It's about Quinn coming home."

"Balderdash." Thomas set his fork on his plate and wiped his mouth with a napkin. "It's about all of us being together for the first time in a decade."

Quinn shifted beside him, a slight frown marring her beautiful features.

A decade? Hadn't Tyler and Gabrielle gotten married last fall? But wait. Quinn and Marshall both had worked eighty-hour weeks for months, trying to make sure everything was perfect on the Lipman campaign. He vaguely remembered her mentioning some family function she was missing to be there.

Surprising that she was even here at all now, much less with a fake boyfriend.

"So." Quinn tapped her fork against the ceramic plate. "What's this news, Shannon?"

"Oh. Well." Shannon stared out toward the ocean. A strand of hair brushed across her cheeks, and Marshall swallowed past the urge to reach across the table and tuck it behind her ear.

This was going to be a long week.

"I've decided to adopt Noah Robinson."

No one said a word, the silence so profound that the cicadas in the yard took up the conversation. Finally, Gabrielle touched Shannon's arm. "That's amazing, Shannon. Congratulations. We'll become mothers together."

Leaning forward to see her from his location on the other side of Gabrielle, Tyler smiled. "He's lucky to have you, sis."

Shannon bit her lip. "I'm the lucky one."

Marshall snuck a peek at Quinn, who wore much the same

look as Shannon had earlier when Quinn was spouting all the good things about her life. Huh. What was the dynamic there?

Something in him just had to let Shannon know, in some small way, that what he'd said earlier was true. That he'd been real, even if she now probably thought him a complete fake. "I think it's fantastic." He cleared his throat. "And very noble of you."

She nodded once, then looked down.

"I've said it before, sweetheart, but we are here if you need us." Genevieve took a sip of water. "I'm not sure how you've managed the application while also juggling the reunion festivities."

"I thought Ashley was the family event planner," Quinn said.

Before Shannon could respond, their mom spoke up again. "Ashley was planning the reunion, but then she started dating Derek Campbell—they got engaged last week—and she asked Shannon to take over."

"Ashley is also in charge of Ben and Bella's wedding next weekend, Mom." Shannon's soft voice seemed to beg for peace.

"I didn't mean to imply she was shirking her duties, dear."

Quinn clucked her tongue. "Guess you miss a lot when you don't live in town anymore."

"You also miss a lot when you never call." Thomas pursed his lips.

"I call." Quinn placed a hand on her father's and smiled up at him. "Just not as often as I'd like. But I miss you every day, Daddy."

Her dad grunted, but something in his eyes softened.

Marshall took a swig of water and shifted in his seat, suddenly warm. With his mom gone for eleven years now and his dad's abandonment a decade before that, family drama was a foreign thing. But however uncomfortable to witness, at least the focus remained firmly off of him and Quinn for the moment.

Genevieve swung her attention back to Shannon. "So how *are* the reunion plans coming?"

"I've actually delegated most of the events to various cousins. Elise, Samantha, and Gabrielle are helping out." Shannon shoved her plate away, her steak only a third eaten. "The adoption stuff has put me a little behind on planning the picnic on Thursday night, but I'll figure it out."

"I'm sure Quinn would love to help, right, dear?" Her mother turned her big blue eyes on her oldest daughter.

"Oh, well, of course, but I still have some work stuff to do while I'm here."

"Surely you can find a few hours."

"I don't think I can, actually." Quinn glanced down at Marshall's hand on the table, then flicked her gaze up at him.

Oh no. He knew that look—the same calculating glimmer she got in her eyes every time she hatched a plan to "catch" a big win at work.

"Babe, would *you* be able to help my sister out? You don't have much else going on this week, right?" She batted her eyes at him.

Did that actually work on other guys?

Marshall tried to shake his head slightly, to communicate with his eyes just how bad of an idea this was. And if Quinn had known about his encounter with Shannon this morning, she'd probably agree with him. "I think your sister would much rather have your help than mine."

But Quinn just laughed and patted him on the arm. "Nonsense. You'll both be fine."

A quick glance at Shannon—at her wide eyes pulsing with some unreadable but intense emotion, mouth shaped like an O, hands wringing her napkin tight—and he guessed she felt anything but "fine" about this situation.

He understood completely.

But before he could protest, Genevieve clapped her hands

together. "It's settled then. Wonderful." She raised a glass of water in a toast. "To a fabulous week of family, friends, and love."

Because he couldn't do anything different, Marshall gritted his teeth and lifted his glass in kind.

CHAPTER 3

*S*he was the very definition of a fool. Look it up in the dictionary—there would be a picture of Shannon Baker. Why had she ever thought Marshall was interested in her? And why hadn't she protested his help last night over dinner?

Shannon picked at a blueberry muffin as her eyes scanned the Frosted Cake from the back corner of the bakery-slash-restaurant. She'd had more than one customer ask if they could steal the second chair from her table since arriving an hour ago —enough time to, hopefully, settle her nerves with a cup of tea and one of Josephine Radcliffe's amazing pastries.

And there was truly no better place to cheer someone up, what with the bright and fun beach decor, the chatter of Sunday brunch-goers, and the morning sunlight filtering through the large bay window that overlooked the beach.

But all the extra time had given her was a twisted-up stomach and sixty minutes of conversing with various locals. Already she'd seen their librarian, Madison, and her boyfriend, Evan, who both smiled like they had a secret, as well as reporter Piper Lansbury, who was making the rounds asking people to

ALL YOU NEED IS LOVE

support the *Walker Beach Press*. Apparently it was in danger of shutting its doors.

And then there was Bud Travis, who'd recently put in a bid for mayor and was out chatting people up. The seventy-year-old already had her vote, but she'd spent a few minutes wishing him well and volunteering her help with his campaign should he need it.

At least those moments had distracted her temporarily from why she was really here.

Every time the bell over the door jangled from across the room, her eyes flicked that way. But still no Marshall. Wasn't like he was all that late, though.

Shannon blew out a steadying breath, took a sip from her lukewarm tea, and picked up a pen, studying the spiral notebook in front of her where she'd written "Family Reunion Picnic Ideas." Every year, they did the same thing. She'd hoped to add her own spin to the event this year, but the rest of the page was still blank.

"Sorry I'm late."

Shannon lurched at the deep baritone echoing from above her, and light brown liquid spilled from her cup across her paper.

"Sorry for that too." Marshall slid into the seat across from her, grabbed several napkins from the dispenser on their table, and helped her dab up the mess. "Didn't mean to startle you."

Her cheeks burned. First she'd dumped a whole bowl of potato salad on her feet last night, now this. "It's my fault." The soaked notebook was ruined. Standing, she walked to the nearest trash can and threw it away, all the while tamping down the urge to run for the Exit.

What was wrong with her? She'd had a very pleasant time with this man just yesterday. He was kind and fun. She had nothing to be nervous about.

But as she approached and he turned his brown eyes on her, her insides turned to ice.

Chill out. He's Quinn's. He wasn't flirting with you yesterday. Just being friendly.

Which meant she had no cause whatsoever to treat him any differently than she had when he'd been a perfect stranger. In fact, she should treat him with even more kindness now that she knew his relationship with her sister.

Marshall pulled a small menu from behind the napkin holder. Today he wore a purple-and-white-striped button-up open over a black shirt. Once again, the shirtsleeves were rolled to his elbows, revealing tan, toned forearms. "So what's good here?"

"Everything."

He nodded at her muffin. "Except the muffins, apparently."

"They're amazing. I'm just not very hungry." With good reason. Being near the man brought a strange mixture of nausea and elation. She pushed the plate across the table. "Try it if you want. I only took a small forkful from that side."

"If you insist." Tugging off a small bit with his fingers, he popped it into his mouth and closed his eyes. "Is this heaven? Wow."

Shannon couldn't hold back a giggle. "Pretty close. You should try Josephine's chocolate croissants."

"I'll be right back then. You want anything else? Another tea?" He leaned down and sniffed the air above the table. "Earl Grey, right?"

The man knew his tea. "Yes. And um, sure." She reached for her purse. "Let me get some cash."

Marshall made a face and waved a hand. "No need. Be right back." He strode toward the front register, where a glass pastry case displayed all of the goodies.

"Hey." A late-twenties brunette wearing a yellow boho tunic stopped by her table, turning a curious eye to Marshall's retreating figure. "I'm surprised to see you here. Doesn't the reunion start today?"

Shannon offered a smile. "Hi, Jenna." Even though they were both Walker Beach natives and in the same grade growing up, she'd never known Jenna Wakefield all that well until Jenna's sister Gabrielle had married Shannon's brother last year. "It starts tonight, but I'm still doing some last-minute planning."

"Is that what we're calling a date now?"

"Oh, this isn't a date." Shannon fisted her hands together under the table. "That's Marshall, Quinn's boyfriend from New York."

Jenna gave a low whistle. "She's got good taste."

Shannon swallowed. "Yeah."

Jenna's dark eyes took her in for a moment, her brow raised. Then she shook her head. "Sorry to interrupt your planning, but I saw you across the room and wanted to ask you if the rumor I heard was true."

"What rumor?"

"About you adopting Noah Robinson."

She sighed. Once a few people knew something in Walker Beach, pretty much everyone did. "Yes, it's true."

Placing a hand on Shannon's shoulder, Jenna smiled. "I think that's great. Not going to lie. Being a single mom is hard." Her ten-year-old son Liam was quiet, but he was a good kid. "If you need any tips about boy mom life or ever just want to commiserate, I'm totally available."

Tears pricked the corners of Shannon's eyes. "Really? Thank you."

"Of course." Jenna's eyes shifted toward the front, where Marshall was headed back, two mugs in hand and a pastry bag tucked beneath his arm. "I'll leave you to your handsome non-date." With a wink, the artsy beauty floated away.

Marshall set the mugs on the table and sat, his nose scrunched. "The owner didn't charge me for any of this."

His incredulous tone made Shannon laugh. "That's Miss Josephine for you." The woman was like a regular Santa Claus, always giving to others with a twinkle in her eye.

"That wouldn't happen back home."

"It's one of the positives of living in a small town."

He took a sip of his tea, the dangling tag declaring it Darjeeling. "One of the only, I imagine."

"What do you have against small towns?"

"Let's just say that I prefer the big city." Cocking his head, he arched an eyebrow. "Have you lived here your whole life?"

"Guilty as charged."

"Then it's hard to explain, but New York has a certain movement to it. It's always awake, always alive. And there, you can be anyone you want to be. People aren't judging you on your family or your past. Just on who you are now. On what you achieve. And you have every opportunity to succeed at the things that *you* choose to make a priority."

"That does sound nice." She tapped the rim of her mug as she cradled it between her hands. "I sometimes dream of moving, of experiencing something different. Being somewhere more cultured, where I could take in art shows and musicals and the opera. And much as I love Miss Josephine's cooking, I've heard the restaurants in New York are to die for."

"Oh man. Yes. And so much variety too. Sushi, Thai, Puerto Rican. I eat a different kind of food every night."

"That would be amazing." And yet ... "I could never leave Walker Beach though. My whole family is here."

"Well, not your *whole* family."

Right. Because Quinn lived across the country. But they hadn't been close in ... well, had they ever, really?

What was she thinking, being this open with Quinn's boyfriend? For all she knew, he'd go back to her sister and spill everything she'd shared, and they'd both have a good laugh over pathetic Shannon Baker and her simple dreams.

The table vibrated and her cousin Ashley's face appeared on the screen of her phone. Probably checking on the status of everything with the reunion. Shannon would call her back later.

She coughed. "Speaking of family, I guess we should get to planning this event."

"Okay, shoot."

And here they were, right back to staring at each other. What was this feeling winding its way up her whole body, tightening her chest, fusing her heart to her ribs, making them ache?

Why, oh why, had Quinn suggested they work together? And why was it so difficult to do? Shannon didn't know this man. Not really.

Then why did it feel like she did?

So many questions and no answers. Nothing that made rational sense anyway.

Shannon blew out a breath, took another sip of tea, and stood, the legs of her chair scraping the wooden floor. "Do you mind if we walk and talk? I process better that way, and I don't want to keep taking up the table since it's so crowded in here."

Marshall didn't bat an eye at her lame excuses, just finished off his own drink, snagged his pastry bag, and stood. "Lead the way."

She did, ignoring all the curious glances from various patrons flung her way. Great. Tongues would be wagging for weeks—Shannon Baker finally somewhere with a man she wasn't related to. She maneuvered past all the customers in the crowded lobby area before emerging into the radiance of another perfect summer day. She hadn't realized how cold the Frosted Cake had been inside until the sun warmed her skin.

Marshall caught up to her and they walked side by side on the sidewalk as she headed south on Main Street. "So, I have to admit, I don't have a ton of experience with event planning."

"Neither do I." They passed her cousin Samantha's Charmed I'm Sure Bookstore, Hardings Market, and Froggies in no time at all. The town was more crowded now than during the week, but still not as busy as last summer before the earthquake that had damaged several buildings in the North Village and all of Walker Beach's economy. Hopefully the upcoming festivals would help jump-start the return of more tourists. "But I'm the one who was available, so Ashley asked me to help out."

"That seems like a lot of pressure."

Shannon shrugged, biting the inside of her cheek to keep her thoughts inside. Because what good would it do to tell him she was terrified of failing the whole family the one time she had something important to do? "We've been doing this family reunion every summer for as long as I can remember. Ashley had a lot of the arrangements made before she handed it off to me, so it shouldn't be too bad. I just got behind." Because organization wasn't her talent.

She didn't really have a talent, to be honest. But she'd help where she could. And her cousin had needed her help, so here she was.

"So what's there left to do? Something about a picnic? Is that like the main event?"

She smiled at the sheriff's wife as they passed on the sidewalk in front of Herman Hardware, which had opened a few months ago after the old hardware store had been converted into the library. "Didn't Quinn prepare you for this week? If not, you might be in for a shock. Our reunion is a whole thing."

He massaged the back of his neck, tugging at the bottom bits of hair curling there. "Quinn didn't tell me a lot of things."

Hmm. Okay, then. Shannon veered down the alley between the hardware store and the edge of the golf course toward one of the least crowded parts of the beach. And yes! Her favorite bench was currently unoccupied, a small miracle at this time of day.

They crossed the sand and sat on the weathered wooden bench, which offered a fantastic view of the ocean in front of them and the grassy green to the left. A golf cart whizzed down the paved path and a pair of golfers chatted at the seventeenth hole, their voices drifting toward Shannon and Marshall, twisting in the breeze so they became unintelligible.

Marshall pulled open the pastry bag and his fingers emerged with a flaky chocolate croissant. Tugging it in half, he offered one piece to Shannon. "You want to fill me in since Quinn was derelict in her duties?"

Quinn, derelict? The description made Shannon grin as she took Marshall's offering. "The reunion kicks off tonight with a burger cookout at the Iridescent Inn, which has been in my family for over a hundred years. My cousin Ben—the one who's getting married next weekend—owns it and his fiancée Bella is the manager there."

"Sounds amazing." He bit into the pastry and groaned. "Kind of like this croissant. You were totally right."

Shannon followed suit, and the combination of salty and sweet burst in her mouth. "Mmm. Yes, I was." She licked her teeth and continued. "Tomorrow it's olallieberry picking in the morning and a family talent show at night. Then there's a Marvel trivia night and a chili and salsa cookout with beach games—volleyball, jet skiing, that sort of thing—on Tuesday and Wednesday. Thursday is our picnic, complete with a fried chicken dinner and games like potato sack races, three-legged races, and cornhole. The Bakers are a rather competitive group."

"Really?" His croissant gone, Marshall dusted his hands free of flaky bits. "Quinn—now that I can believe. But you don't strike me as the type."

"Maybe I would be." She lifted a shoulder and tried for a smile. Tried, and failed. "But after a while, you stop trying to compete when you know the inevitable outcome."

"And what's that?" His brow crinkled as he turned his body slightly toward her.

The very edges of their knees touched for a moment before

Shannon swung hers to face forward completely. "Quinn always wins." Her voice nearly choked on the words—so often thought, so rarely spoken.

And here she was speaking them to the one person she shouldn't.

Shannon folded her arms over her chest and chewed her fingernail. "Anyway, the rest of the weekend will be full of wedding festivities, and the reunion finishes up on the Fourth of July at the town's Fireworks Festival. Everyone goes home after that."

"Sounds like a really fun time."

"It is."

When he didn't say anything more in response, she braved a glance. Just like yesterday morning on the beach, he looked at her in a way that turned her inside out—like he saw her. The real her. The one she rarely let anyone see, mostly because they didn't seem interested, or even aware that the Shannon she projected wasn't always the Shannon she held tucked away close in her heart.

It's all in your mind. Because he was Quinn's man, and Shannon would never in a million years try to steal him from her sister.

It would be wrong—and she'd never succeed.

When Quinn had joked that her family made up half the town, she might not have been exaggerating.

Marshall tried to ignore his pounding temple as he focused on what his fake girlfriend's uncle—Frank?—was saying.

"The economy has finally started to pick up around here." Even though they stood in a group of eight or ten, the well-built man in his fifties directed his thoughts toward Quinn's older cousin, Ben, the owner of the inn where the opening reunion night was in full swing. "Your friend Evan has done good work on that front."

"Agreed." Ben, a six-foot-something guy with broad shoulders and one arm slung around a stylish brunette with blonde highlights, took a swig of Coke. "He's hopeful that the Christmas festival will continue to bring in sponsorships and money to help the local businesses recover."

Marshall had no idea what they were talking about, but what was new? For the last hour, he'd met and conversed with at least fifty members of the Baker family, including the Griffin sextuplets who were second cousins on Quinn's great-aunt's side. Pretty sure, anyway. And there were at least fifty more he'd yet to meet.

The aroma of burgers wafted from the corner of the courtyard, where Tyler, his dad, and a few other people manned the grills. On the other side of them, a wrought iron gate stood open, revealing a path that led down to a gorgeous private beach. Some members of the Baker clan had already headed that way, but most stood inside the courtyard, sipping on drinks and laughing as they waited for dinner to be served.

Not for the first time, his eyes wandered upward from his place in the stone courtyard to take in the two-story Iridescent Inn. The charming B&B was a nice mix of historic and modern, with wooden clapboard siding, a wraparound upper porch with a staircase that descended into the courtyard, and pale blue paint that appeared somehow fresh, not worn down by the wind and sand and other elements at constant work here.

Quinn's fingernails dug into Marshall's palm as she tugged on his hand. "Babe? Did you hear my cousin?"

"Oh." He maneuvered his gaze back to Ben. "Sorry, what's that?"

The crowd chuckled. He'd definitely missed something.

"Not *that* cousin." Quinn rolled her eyes, her giggle grating against the pounding in Marshall's head. "Cameron."

And which one was that again?

A guy with blond curls and a deep tan, wearing blue board shorts and a white T-shirt, waved his hand, a huge grin plastered across his face. Oh yeah, one of the sextuplets. "Right? We're a lot to take in, dude. I just wondered if this was your first visit to California."

Normally, Marshall had no problem with small talk. After all, it was part of being in the corporate world—especially the marketing world. But this mixture of trying to be himself without giving away that he and Quinn weren't actually an item had him second-guessing almost everything he said.

Not to mention the fact that Cameron's question instantly led to thoughts of Dad—and the reason Marshall had avoided the West Coast at all costs until now.

The blood in his veins buzzed, rushing through his ears to a distracting degree. "Yes." He waited for a beat, then added, "It's beautiful, though."

Quinn squeezed his hand, gentler this time, and her smile indicated he'd done well.

For now. But he had a whole week left of this charade and was already worn thin over the deception. That didn't bode well for his ability to maintain their story without cracking.

Of course, being around a certain blonde all morning hadn't helped. In reality, that's when his headache had begun. Shannon was just so ... guileless, so sweet. Why hadn't she totally filleted him for flirting with her on the beach when, by all appearances, he was in a serious relationship? Any other woman of his acquaintance would have done so with no problem. Either that, or they'd have turned the flirting up a notch to try to steal him away.

Maybe that's why he found himself so attracted to Shannon. Not just the innocence surrounding her whole being, but how different she was.

And that was exactly the line of thinking that was going to

get him into trouble. Because he found himself wanting to tell her the truth about his relationship with Quinn, but he couldn't fully trust that she wouldn't reveal it to Quinn's whole family. And that would leave Marshall no closer to the director position than before.

He simply needed to stay as far away from her as he could.

Quinn's family picked up their conversation again, this time discussing all the improvements Ben and Bella had made to the inn in the last year since an earthquake had damaged it. Marshall leaned close to Quinn and lowered his voice. "I'm going to get some air for a minute. Be right back."

"All right, but don't leave me alone for too long. This isn't fun for me either."

He grunted his assurance and headed for the door leading inside the inn. With such amazing weather—seventy-something at the moment and the sun headed for the horizon, promising an even cooler late evening—finding anyone inside was unlikely. Maybe he could find a quiet corner where his head would stop screaming at him.

The white door creaked as he opened it into what appeared to be the inn's kitchen. Unlike the outside of the place, the kitchen seemed in dire need of an update—its cabinets boasted peeling paint, and a pale green refrigerator with rounded edges sat in the corner.

But it wasn't empty as he'd thought. His eyes settled upon a very surprised Shannon, if her wide eyes and slack jaw were any indications. She stood over a small table in the eat-in kitchen space, a cookie in each hand. At least a dozen dessert platters containing an assortment of brownies, cookies, and little fruit-filled pastries covered the table. A partially filled plate sat directly in front of her.

"Hey." He should go, but instead Marshall found himself shutting the door behind him, blocking out the noise of the reunion. The peace of the kitchen immediately filled his lungs.

Okay, he'd only stay a minute or two.

Shannon placed the two Oreo-looking cookies onto the platter. "Hi." In white shorts and a hot-pink ruffled top, hair pulled back in a loose braid, and simple hoop earrings adorning her ears, she looked sweetly sexy. "What are you doing in here?"

"I could ask you the same thing." He shuffled across the white tile floor toward her. "The party's out there."

"Yes, I know." Her tone teased him. Despite her initial reaction, maybe she was getting comfortable with him after all. "I helped to plan it, remember?" With movements that seemed effortless, she pulled desserts from each plate and, one at a time, consolidated them onto the platter in front of her.

He cocked his head as he drew nearer, breathing in the scent of sugar and flour and ... was that watermelon? He'd noticed the smell earlier today, taunting him as the breeze had blown up off the water to where they'd sat on the bench, planning Thursday's picnic. She must use a fruit-scented shampoo or something. Marshall got the strangest urge to wrap his arms around her from behind and nuzzle his nose into her hair.

But he wasn't creepy like that, so he stayed put.

"Can I help you with something?" She glanced up at him, her nose scrunched.

Whoa. He was way closer than he'd intended to be. Taking a step back, he plucked a cookie from the plate. "I needed a breather."

"Didn't your mother ever tell you dessert would spoil your dinner?" Her lips quirked as she continued working.

"She did." Thinking about his mom, even for a moment, pinched his chest. "But would it surprise you to learn that I didn't listen?"

Shannon glanced up at him, pushing a tendril of hair that had fallen from her braid out of her face. "Actually, yes. You seem like the kind of guy who follows the rules."

If only she knew ...

What would she say if he told her why he was really here?

She'd never talk to him again, that's what. And he'd lose his shot at having Quinn's recommendation.

Needing a distraction, Marshall took a bite of the cookie in his hand, then immediately groaned.

"What's wrong?"

"Nothing worse than getting oatmeal raisin when you were expecting chocolate chip."

Shannon's laugh lilted through the kitchen, through Marshall's whole being, and he realized his headache was no more. Something about watching her nimble fingers work, about just being in her presence, was more effective than ibuprofen.

What *was* she doing? As he finished off his cookie and watched her work in silence, he saw a pattern emerge on the platter. She'd taken darker desserts and used them to create a starburst that began at the center and worked its way outward in rays like the sun.

"I've never seen such artistry in cookie plating before."

She shrugged a shoulder, feigning nonchalance—but her reddening cheeks gave away her pleasure at his compliment. "I know we could put the platters out as they are, but I want everything to look as pretty as possible. After all, it's a special time."

"I'd offer to help, but I'm afraid I'd do just the opposite."

"No worries. I'm almost done."

Quirking an eyebrow, he pivoted and glanced around the kitchen. How had he not noticed the platters sitting on the countertop before now? Walking over, he examined them, each one with a different design—flowers, hearts, diamonds, and more.

"These are great." He turned back to face her. "But doesn't it bother you that your family probably won't even notice the patterns?"

"I'm used to it." Shannon gave a sad smile before returning her attention to the last platter. "Besides, that's not why I do it."

"So why then?" Marshall pulled out a chair and sat in it backward, looping his arms over the top and setting his chin on the top of his hands.

Pausing, Shannon fixed him with a stare, her lips swung to the side, forehead crinkled in what appeared to be concentration. "It's enough to simply create beauty. It doesn't matter if no one else acknowledges it. That doesn't change the fact it's there."

He whistled. Beautiful *and* deep. "I like that sentiment." Marshall scrubbed his hand across his jaw. "It's just so different from the way I was raised."

"And how was that?"

"My dad didn't really care about making things beautiful. He's an attorney and used to be a state senator, which of course is a lot to live up to. And he was always pushing me to be better, to achieve more." Marshall paused, an ache he'd shoved down more times than he could count re-emerging to rub his heart raw. "I'm his only kid, so I get it. But he was always riding my tail, until …"

Shannon glanced up. But instead of prying, she simply looked at him, eyes soft, offering comfort without the necessity of words. Then she went back to busying her hands.

What was wrong with him? He never talked about this.

Marshall cleared his throat. "Anyway, I admire you and your talents. I don't have an artistic bone in my body."

Shannon moved to the kitchen, opened a drawer, and pulled out a cardboard rectangular tube. "Thankfully, you don't have to be artistic to use plastic wrap."

Grinning, he popped up from the chair and snagged the yellow box from her hands. "Aye, aye, captain."

While she finished situating the rest of the cookies on her platter, he wrapped the others with plastic.

"So why did you need a breather earlier? Overwhelmed at the sheer volume of Bakers?"

"Yes. Totally. How do you keep them all straight?"

"It helps that I've lived here my whole life and they're *my* family." She placed the last brownie on the platter, nodded, and dusted her hands together. "Besides, it's all I know. They're all I know. What about you? You said you were an only child?"

"Yeah, so all of this is the exact opposite of what *I* know." The plastic crinkled against his fingertips as he stretched it across a glass platter. "I always wanted a brother or sister—even a cousin —but it was just me, my dad, and my mom. Then they divorced when I was eleven, and my mom and I moved to New York City to live in the house my grandparents left her when they died."

He opened his mouth to finish the story—Mom's car accident when he was twenty, Dad's subsequent move to Los Angeles—but stopped. What was he doing, telling her his life story when they'd just met?

But Shannon took the information in stride, not flashing him pitying looks like he'd half expected. "I guess we're always uncomfortable with what we aren't used to. I wouldn't know what to do without a crowd to hide me away."

The teeth of the cardboard tube grated against his finger as he tore off a long piece of plastic. "No offense, but you don't exactly blend into the crowd."

When she didn't answer, he peeked at her. She stood stock-still, hands frozen in the air, hovering above the platter, her eyes locked on him, the strangest look on her face.

Maybe awe? Confusion? A tinge of anger?

Uh oh. What had he said?

He forced a chuckle. "Well, it looks like we've got enough cookies to feed an army. And I'm guessing those burgers are just about done, so ..."

For a moment, Shannon didn't move. She swallowed hard.

But then her trance cleared. "Right. If you don't mind, let's move some onto the dessert table set up outside."

"Sounds good."

They each gathered up a few platters, and he followed her through the door. Instead of having dispersed, the crowd stood in mostly silence, riveted on a man and woman standing on a couple of chairs in the center of the courtyard.

The woman looked a lot like Shannon, with blonde hair that fell to the center of her back, but she was taller and built more like an athlete. The guy, whose hand she clutched in her own, had dark hair and a beard, and he stared down at the woman with all the love and affection a man could possibly have for a woman.

The way Marshall's dad used to look at his mom. Before.

He shook off the thought and zeroed in on what the blonde was saying. "I know this will come as a surprise to you all, but last night, Derek and I eloped!" The crowd erupted into applause and whispers of surprise, but they quieted down again when the woman started speaking. "Don't worry, we'll still have a reception this winter—after the vineyard harvest, of course— but we just couldn't wait to start our lives together."

Then she turned and kissed the man deep and long. More hoots and hollers broke loose from the Baker clan.

Shannon slipped through the crowd, heading for a folding table with a big empty spot. Marshall followed.

After setting down her two platters, she pushed the heel of her hand against her eye. Whoa, was she crying?

He placed his platters next to hers. "Hey, you okay?"

"Me? Oh yeah, fine." Shannon's smile wobbled.

He shouldn't touch her—not with the way his arms itched to pull her against his chest—but he couldn't help his hand cradling her elbow as he tugged her away from the crowd. "What's wrong?"

For a moment, she didn't speak, just shook her head. "That

ALL YOU NEED IS LOVE

was my cousin Ashley and her fiancé—husband—Derek. She called me after you and I met this morning and told me about her elopement. But hearing it again, out loud ..."

"Do you not like the guy or something?"

"Oh no! He's great, and perfect for her." She sniffed. "I just wish I could have been there, you know? She said it was because she didn't want to distract me from the reunion planning. That's why she asked Madison and Evan to stand up for them. But she's not just my cousin. She's also one of my best friends, like the sister I never had."

Her hand flew to her mouth as her eyes widened. "I mean, I know I have a sister, but ..." A grimace crossed her face.

Marshall's thoughts warred with each other. He wanted to lean in, to tell her that it was okay—her secrets, her thoughts, were safe with him. But he also knew what was wiser. He wasn't here to get involved in family drama. To care. To get attached.

It wasn't his business.

His business was to get that job promotion. Because what else did he have? Everything else he'd cared about had been taken from him. Work was the one thing he could control.

And anything resembling love ... well, love wasn't worth the risk.

Still, the tears shining in Shannon's eyes tugged at him.

"There you are, babe." Quinn's voice jerked him out of his musings. "What happened to that fresh air you were looking for?"

Shannon retreated toward the safety of the kitchen. Didn't take a genius to see that she and Quinn were at odds. Maybe even that Shannon somehow saw herself as inferior to Quinn.

Which, frankly, was ridiculous.

You don't care, remember?

Pushing a deep puff of air from his lips, Marshall looped his arm around Quinn's waist. "Sorry about that. I'm good now. Lead on."

CHAPTER 4

*T*his … now this was the life.

What more could she possibly need?

Shannon plucked a plump olallieberry—a cross between blackberries, dewberries, and raspberries—from its bush and popped it between her lips. The sweet-tart juice squirted in all directions inside her mouth. "Mmm."

Beside her, Noah reached into the bush and pulled out a handful of the black-colored berries. They'd only been here for thirty minutes and already his lips were stained red. "Told you they were yummy, Miss Shannon." Instead of putting them into the plastic-lined bucket they were sharing, he stuck the whole handful in his mouth.

"You've got to put some in the bucket, bud. Otherwise we won't have enough for me to make you a pie." Shannon tousled his hair.

Spread out in the fields around her, various family members worked together to fill their own buckets. The farm where they'd scheduled an exclusive picking time on the second day of the reunion sat just south of town, adjacent to the Olallieberry Canyon area just off Highway 1.

A breeze rustled the leaves of the junipers sitting atop the rolling hills that overlooked the rows of olallieberry bushes. Shannon followed Noah, content to just watch him kneeling in the dirt, his bare toes getting filthy in his flip-flops. His enthusiasm knew no bounds, and she had difficulty keeping pace with him as he darted in and out of the rows.

Stopping at a bush sagging with an inordinate amount of berries, she squatted and breathed deeply of the cleansing air, which hinted at the ocean brine just a mile or so away.

Noah's laughter floated back to her, good medicine for her soul—and today she was one step closer to becoming his mom forever. Just this morning, she'd heard from the foster care agency again and learned that they had time to conduct her interview tomorrow morning. Shannon had already told her parents she'd have to forego the family hike at ten.

"Hey!" Noah shouted from farther down her row. "Marshall!"

Jerking her head toward his voice and pivoting to stand at the same time threw off her center of balance—and oh so gracefully, Shannon fell headlong into the bush. Fine sharp points pricked the undersides of her forearms as a garbled squeak flew from her mouth.

"Whoa. You all right?" Strong arms first steadied her then hauled her backward and onto her feet.

She glanced up into Marshall's eyes, and this close she could make out the golden rims ringing the brown center like an inside out caramel. "Y-yeah." Stepping back, she examined her palms and other places where the plant had scratched her. No blood, thankfully, just irritating little scrapes quickly turning pink. "Thanks."

"No problem." Tilting his head, Marshall lifted his fingers and lightly grazed her right cheek.

She winced at the contact.

"You're hurt."

"It's nothing."

Frowning, Marshall reached into his pocket and pulled out a napkin. "Here." He hesitated then pressed the napkin softly against the skin just below her cheekbone. The warmth of his fingers bled through the paper.

Their interaction in the kitchen last night—the one that had played on a loop in her mind—returned to this moment. *"No offense, but you don't exactly blend into the crowd."* She'd held each word close, broken them apart, put them back together, and still, the meaning eluded her.

Because what it *seemed* to mean couldn't be what it really meant.

He was Quinn's boyfriend. Why would he be looking twice at Shannon?

This was wrong, on so many levels. He was just a nice guy, and Shannon was making an idiot of herself.

Her fingers secured the napkin before she stepped away. "Thanks again. Are you having fun? Where's Quinn?" The words tumbled from her lips, but they were necessary.

"You're welcome. Yes, a blast. And she had enough of nature and headed back to the farm store for some coffee." Marshall's lips quirked into a grin.

"That sounds like her." Together, they both walked toward Noah, who had joined up with her cousin Sophie's two boys, Brodie and Brogan. The kids were tossing berries into the air and trying to catch them in their mouths, succeeding only half the time.

Marshall interrupted them. "You guys want to know the secret to catching those every time?"

"Yes!"

He taught them how to keep their elbow at their waists and use it like a hinge before flicking their hands quickly upward. Sophie's boys caught on quickly, cheering as they landed berry after berry, but Noah failed several times in a row.

The five-year-old crossed his arms and stomped on the dropped berries, sending red and purple juice squirting into the dirt. "I don't want to play this stupid game anymore."

She'd seen him get like this before. His perfectionist tendencies often made failures seem bigger than they really were, and his MO was to give up instead of keep trying. But before she could launch into a round of encouragement, Marshall crouched, getting eye to eye with Noah.

Meanwhile, Brodie and Brogan ran off to show Sophie their latest trick.

"Little man, you're doing awesome. Do you know how many times it took me to get this right? I didn't do it perfectly the first time either."

"Really?"

"Yeah, really. My dad taught me, but it took lots of practice before I got it right. And when I finally did, I was so proud to show him." Marshall helped Noah position his arm at his waist, then mimicked the flicking motion. "You might not be able to control how good you are at something, but if you never give up, if you keep practicing, I promise you'll get it eventually."

Warmth flooded her chest at the sincerity in his tone and the memory of what he'd shared about his dad yesterday. He hadn't gone into details, but she'd sensed more to the story—much more. And even though she'd longed to learn more about Marshall St. John, a warning had flashed in her brain, stopping her from asking.

She'd been in dangerous territory then, and she was in dangerous territory now.

Noah tried again, but failed once more. He squinted at the berry on the ground, then moved his gaze to Marshall. "Can I practice by myself for a while?"

"Of course. Just holler if you need us."

Turning, Marshall picked up Noah and Shannon's bucket, which was woefully low on berries. "I'll help you fill this puppy up in no time." Before she could protest, he'd placed his hand on her lower back and guided her away from Noah.

Shannon shuffled down the path, kicking up bits of dirt. "You were really great with him." He'd make an amazing father someday. Maybe he and Quinn would have babies together.

The thought soured the sweet berries in her stomach.

No, no, no. This couldn't be happening. What was the matter with her? But as much as she'd tried to deny it, Shannon was the worst kind of person—the kind with a crush on her sister's boyfriend.

She had to nip this in the bud, and there was one sure way to do that. Stopping beside a bush bursting with olallieberries, she sat on the ground and busied her hands with picking. "So tell me about you and Quinn."

"Uh." Marshall lowered himself next to her, placing the bucket between them. "What do you want to know?"

Nothing. The plink of the berries falling into the metal bucket filled the silence while Shannon concocted a response. "What attracted you to her? Besides the fact she's gorgeous, of course."

Her heart inexplicably picked up speed. Why did his answer matter so much? Shannon attempted to steady her trembling fingers as she tugged berries off their thick, woody stems.

"I don't know." Marshall made quick work of the harvest.

Down the lane, a chicken clucked. Overhead, a cloud obscured the sun for a brief moment. And still Marshall didn't give more of an answer.

It was none of her business. She shouldn't have asked. And yet, much as she didn't want to know, some part of her wondered. Maybe he saw something in her sister that Shannon herself had missed—a softness, a vulnerability. Something other than the hard edges and full-blown confidence Quinn had displayed all her life.

Well, there was that bit of time after the car accident she and Mom were in when Quinn was nine—the one that had left her with a scar on her face and the need for multiple plastic surgeries. After a small battle with depression, Quinn had refused to let the scar bother her, becoming the person she was today.

Hmm.

Shannon glanced over at him.

He was staring at her, his mouth screwed up on one side. "Shannon..."

"Yeah?"

"Me and Quinn ... well, it's complicated." Marshall's mouth opened, then snapped shut again. Sighing, he nudged the mostly full bucket closer to her and stood. "And speaking of Quinn, I'd better go find her."

He trudged down the lane, leaving Shannon with a twisted stomach. Had she revealed too much in their conversation?

Her hand caught up several berries from the top layer in the bucket and she closed her fist over them, squishing the fruit. Red juice dripped through her fingers into the dirt.

Ugh. She really needed to get her thoughts under control. The focus of the next twenty-four hours especially had to remain on Noah, on tomorrow's interview ... on the things that she could actually have.

A week ago, he'd been buried in work, digging through pages of ideas he'd scrawled to find the perfect one to pitch a cable company.

But tonight, Marshall dug through a pile of costumes that had been dumped in a side room off the auditorium of Piedras Blancas Church. Sequined skirts, a pale green blazer, a couple of clown noses, a variety of wigs, and other ragtag pieces of clothing adorned the floor. Several members of the Baker family buzzed in and out of the room while Marshall examined his choices.

How had he let Quinn talk him into performing at her family reunion's talent show? Sure, he sang at karaoke bars all the time as a way to let off steam, but that didn't mean he wanted to perform in front of people he actually knew. Or was getting to know, anyway.

Guess he'd found out just how far he was willing to go for this promotion—in addition to lying to an amazing woman and her family, of course.

Groaning, Marshall bent to pick up a hot-pink feather boa.

"Not sure that's exactly your color, Sinatra."

As he turned, Marshall found Shannon leaning against the doorway, a clipboard clutched to her chest and a wry grin affixed to her lips. With a black flowy skirt and dark blue lacy tank, her hair down and curled, she was gorgeous. But then, from what he'd seen, the woman always looked that way, even if she wore simple shorts and a T-shirt like she had at the olallieberry fields this morning.

Man, he'd been so close to spilling the truth then. It had taken all of his self-control to get up and leave her there, but he still didn't know what she would do with the information if he told her.

Sure, if he didn't get this promotion, he'd get the next one. But he *deserved* this one. Had worked endlessly for it. And yeah, maybe the validation wouldn't be bad either. But it wasn't about that—at least, he didn't think so.

It was about work being a sure thing, the thing that wouldn't fail him, the thing he could pour into and get a visible return on. This nebulous *something* he felt when he was with Shannon, on the other hand ... who knew where that would lead?

He couldn't risk all his hard work for a woman, no matter how sweet and kind and ... alluring.

Ignoring the path of his thoughts, Marshall looped the feather boa around his neck and struck a pose—hands on his hips, nose in the air. "Not my color? You sure?"

"Hmm." Shannon tapped her chin with a pen she'd pulled off the clipboard. "I take it back. It's perfect." Then she moved toward the costume pile and unearthed a top hat, which she set on his head. "But this might be more your style."

He lowered the brim like a cowboy. "Thank you kindly, ma'am." His eyes searched the costume pile until he found what he sought—a black curved hat with a large silver flower on one side. Marshall turned and plunked it on Shannon's head. "There. Now you just need one of those flapper outfits from the twenties and you could be my co-star."

He'd said it as a joke, but something about the idea held appeal. Even though it was a terrible idea.

Tempting. But terrible.

Shannon scrambled to remove the hat, smoothing her hair with the hand not clutching the clipboard. "Oh no. I don't sing. I'm just the stage manager tonight." Then she pivoted and exited the room.

Marshall checked his watch. The talent show should be starting any minute. About fifteen acts had volunteered—or been volunteered—and the rest of the family would sit in the audience of the church, where Shannon's cousin Spencer Griffin was pastor.

"She says she doesn't sing, but that's a lie."

Marshall jumped at the intrusion and swiveled to find Shannon's cousin Ashley emerging from the room next door that was serving as the ladies' dressing room.

Rustles and giggles floated from the other side of the door. Quinn had wandered back there about fifteen minutes ago to change into her floor-length gown. Apparently she was a trained vocalist.

Being a diva definitely seemed right up her alley.

But Shannon too? Talent must run in the family. "Is that right?"

The diamond on Ashley's left hand caught a shine under the church's fluorescent lighting. "I don't know how much interaction you've had with my cousin yet, but she's basically the most humble person you'll ever meet."

His fingers twisted around the boa, which still hung from his neck. The feathers tickled his palms. "I gathered that."

"I've only heard her sing in the car, but that girl's got skill." Ashley tugged at the tips of her hair, cocking her head as she sighed. "I just wish our whole family could see the hidden star that Shannon is."

Him too. "Maybe you could convince her to perform."

Ashley toed the pile of clothing at her feet. "I wish I could. But she'd never have the confidence to go up there by herself. Especially with Quinn performing." Her lips pursed. "Oops. Forget I said that." She hurried from the room, the black tap shoes on her feet clattering as she went.

Marshall slipped the feather boa back into the pile, adjusted the top hat, and snagged a black, sequined blazer that was a size too big for him. As he eased it on, he couldn't help but wonder … Shannon's speaking voice soothed his soul. What would it sound like backed by music?

Breathy and light?

Low and throaty?

Electric?

Shaking his head, he left the room and moved toward the auditorium down the hall. Marshall peeked inside and estimated about fifty percent of the wooden pews were filled. The scent of popcorn permeated the air, and several people munched on the snack. Up front, Shannon spoke with a tech guy in black, nodding at something he was saying.

The man handed her a microphone then left her standing

there alone. Her lips turned down and she fled the small stage. At the bottom, she shoved the mic into the hands of a woman with long red hair wearing a brown hippie skirt and white tank —Jules, if he remembered correctly from the introductions last night.

Supposedly she was Quinn and Shannon's aunt, but she didn't look a day over forty. The woman hugged Shannon and strode up onto the stage without hesitation. "Hey, family! Welcome to the annual Baker Reunion Talent Show!"

The audience clapped and whistled then quieted while Jules explained how the night would work. Marshall settled himself against the back wall, while most of the other performers sat in a designated row. He didn't see Quinn, but maybe she was still getting ready.

Jules introduced the first act, two teenage girl cousins doing a scene from some movie Marshall didn't recognize. He laughed along with the crowd at their antics. Then came a magic show by Mark West, Shannon and Quinn's uncle.

The next time Jules got onstage, she introduced "everyone's favorite star—Quinn Baker!"

Quinn strutted up the three steps toward center stage, her whole body sheathed in a tight, deep purple gown that sparkled under the lights. Her hair was swept back from her face, which was partially covered in a mask on the right side, and elbow-length black gloves covered her hands and forearms.

Dark and deep music drifted from the speakers, a song Marshall recognized from the one time he'd seen *The Phantom of the Opera* on Broadway when a grateful client had sent the firm tickets. In smooth tones, Quinn sang about the music of the night.

Interesting choice. Instead of the character he'd expected her to perform—Christine, the lead female—she'd chosen to voice the phantom, a lonely creature yearning for love.

Okay, he was definitely reading too much into that one. Except the woman had been dumped just a few days ago. Maybe she really did feel more deeply than she let on.

His eyes drifted from Quinn toward the spot where Shannon stood just offstage, arms folded across her chest. Even from across the room, Marshall caught the tension in her posture, the cut in her gaze.

And when Quinn finished, flourishing a curtsy, and the crowd erupted in applause, Shannon pushed her fingers underneath her eyes.

"I'm used to it." From what he could tell, Shannon kept to the background on purpose. Who knew why? Maybe he'd never know. But in this moment, he couldn't help but want everyone else to see what it had taken him only minutes to observe.

And maybe he could.

He shouldn't.

But ...

Before he could talk himself out of it, Marshall left the room, grabbed what he needed, then headed back to chat with the tech guys for a moment. Finally, he crossed the room to meet Shannon where she stood while her cousin Cameron performed a comedy routine.

"Hey."

Was it just him or had her eyes brightened at his whispered greeting? Could have been the lights. "You're up next. You ready?" She eyed the feathers in his hands. "Decided to jazz things up a bit, did you?"

"You have no idea. But this isn't for me. It's for you. Thought you could use a little decoration." He placed the boa around her neck.

"I'm just the stage manager." Her jaw flexed as if she were trying not to smile.

Not tonight. He leaned in closer on instinct. "By the way, I'm switching songs at the last minute."

Her eyebrows lifted. "Really? What song?"

"'Ain't No Mountain High Enough.'"

"Ooo, good choice. I love that song."

"I was hoping you'd say that." Ignoring her scrunched nose, he just smiled and turned his attention back to the stage.

Cameron ended his set, thanking the crowd and blowing exaggerated kisses. From the front row, Quinn caught Marshall's eyes and shot him a thumbs-up.

His throat tingled.

Terrible, terrible idea.

He side-eyed Shannon. Terrible ... but totally worth it.

Jules breezed past them and exchanged places with Cameron. "As always, thank you to Cam for providing some much-needed laughter." She waited until the crowd's snickers died down. "Next up, we have a newbie to our little reunion—though who knows. Someday he might be a regular part of the lineup."

Sheesh. Marshall barely held back an inner groan. Shannon shifted from one foot to the other beside him.

"Please welcome to the stage our lovely Quinn's boyfriend, Mr. Marshall St. John!"

"Break a leg," Shannon said as he walked away from her.

She might want to *actually* break his leg after what he was about to pull. He snagged the microphone from Jules and waited for her to exit the stage. "Thank you everyone for having me. I can't tell you how much fun I'm having here with you all."

Okay, fun was stretching it, but they *were* nice people and under normal circumstances—aka not lying—he might be having fun.

"I love being up here too, but tonight I want to invite someone to the stage for a duet."

Some aahs echoed from the crowd. Great. They thought he was asking Quinn. And Quinn herself looked at him sideways but, smile plastered to her lips, started to stand.

He hurried toward stage right, walked down the steps, and offered his hand to Shannon. "Shannon Baker, will you sing with me?"

She shrank back, hands firmly gripping the boa around her neck, stretching it so tight he thought it might snap. "What? No."

Marshall held the microphone up to his mouth and turned to the crowd. "A little bird told me that Shannon here is an amazing singer, but seems she's a bit shy and could use some encouragement."

Her family applauded and cheered. "Come on, Shannon! You've got this!"

Shannon licked her lips and shook her head. "I can't."

"You can do this," Marshall said off mic. "Come on. I'll be with you every step of the way. Ain't no mountain high, right?" Once again, he held out his hand.

Shannon stared at it.

She was going to turn him down, make him look like an idiot.

Maybe he was one.

But before he knew what was happening, she'd slipped her hand inside his and fireworks exploded in his chest. He wanted to lean in and touch her forehead with his own, to whisper his confidence in her. But that would be much too intimate and look much worse than asking his "girlfriend's" sister to sing with him instead of his girlfriend herself.

Together, they climbed the stage, and Marshall unhooked a second microphone from the stand to the left and handed it to Shannon. The upbeat music threaded through the auditorium. Shannon stood straight as a queen, eyes unblinking as they took in the audience. Hers seemed to land on Quinn, whose frown was as big as one of the billboards in Times Square.

Oh well. Too late to back out now.

Marshall started in, crooning the first few lines until it was Shannon's turn.

As if finally realizing what was happening, she sputtered out a line or two, her voice soft, brittle, choked.

How could he get her to relax into this? Maybe if she forgot about the crowd, her nerves would dissipate.

Crossing the stage, he snagged her hand again and turned her to face him—only him. Marshall smiled at her while she finished squeaking out her solo. Squeezing her hand, he launched into the chorus.

And slowly, magically, she started to follow. Started to lean into the music, to loosen.

To soar.

Ashley had been right. The girl could sing.

A smile as wide as the rivers they sang about overtook Shannon's face. She even swayed in time to the beat, finally dropping his hand and using it to clutch her heart, to emphasize the words, showcasing her sassiness and talent and … joy.

As the music faded from the room and the sound of wild applause swooped in, Marshall's breath came heavy and strong. After their bows, he tugged her offstage and then couldn't help wrapping her into the curve of his embrace. Hopefully the continued roar of the crowd covered the erratic beating of his heart.

When he pulled back, Shannon looked up at him. "Thank you for that." She bit her lip and, aw man—he wanted to kiss her.

This was crazy. He'd known her what? Three days?

But before he could act on his more-than-idiotic impulse, someone dragged his arm away from Shannon—and he was staring at Quinn. "Great job, babe. I knew you were talented, but that was quite. The. Performance." She spoke through gritted teeth.

And then she kissed him.

What? No!

Marshall placed both of his hands on Quinn's upper arms and pulled back, staring down at her smug grin.

And as his eyes scanned the room, all he caught of Shannon was a flash of blonde hair disappearing into the hallway.

CHAPTER 5

*T*his morning was soooo not the time for a lack-of-sleep headache.

But it seemed Shannon's body didn't care that the foster care agency's social worker would arrive for her interview any minute. Her temples went right on throbbing.

Groaning, she flopped onto the edge of her lavender couch, accidentally pulling a folded quilt from its spot on the worn arm. Lucky trotted over and placed his head in Shannon's lap, whining to show his sympathy.

"Whatever." She leaned down and touched her nose to his. "You slept hard all night. I heard you rumbling away."

Lucky's snores had served as background music for the movie playing over and over in Shannon's head—the one where she had been the star for once.

And, oh yeah, had also totally embarrassed herself in front of the entire family.

It hadn't mattered that after her and Marshall's performance, she'd been overrun with compliments from cousins, uncles, aunts, her parents, and her grandma. She'd seen the accusation in Quinn's eyes right before she'd very obviously claimed her man with a kiss.

Thing was, Quinn had been one hundred percent right.

"I should have said no to the whole thing, right, Luck?" And yet, it had felt good to sing in front of everyone. Scary, but good.

Even better to sing with Marshall.

Her stomach grumbled, protesting Shannon's lack of breakfast. But with an hour of sleep before her alarm had angrily awakened her this morning, she'd pushed Snooze one too many times before realizing the social worker was due to arrive in thirty minutes—barely enough time to shower, get dressed, and blow-dry her hair.

She glanced at the distressed vintage-looking white clock above her television. The social worker would be here in about five minutes. Maybe she could just ease back and close her eyes …

Insistent knocking and a bark made her jolt. Shannon's eyes burned with dryness. What was going on?

Shannon glanced at the clock. Five minutes past nine. Oh no. She must have fallen asleep.

Lucky paced at the top of the stairs, which led down to her front door. The ringing of the doorbell echoed through the apartment, and more knocking followed.

Someone was definitely here. The social worker. How long had she left him standing out there?

Bolting to her feet, she stumbled, grabbing her still aching head. Shannon took Lucky by the collar, shoved him into her bedroom, and hurried down the stairs to the front door where she found a scowling middle-aged man with a phone against his ear.

He shoved the device into his pocket. "Are you Shannon Baker?"

"I am. And I'm so sorry to keep you waiting."

The squat man wore a short-sleeved, button-up shirt tucked

sloppily into khakis, and his right hand clutched a file folder. "I've been standing here for five minutes and thought I must have the wrong place. Of course, all of these condos look the same."

His nose wrinkled as he looked past her. All that was visible at the moment was worn carpet and family pictures lining the walls as the stairs ascended.

"Sorry again. Please come in." Shannon stepped aside. "Mr. Peters, isn't it?" How her muddled brain had managed to remember that, she had no clue, but she shot up a prayer of thanks.

"Yes. Arnold Peters." He stood there, obviously waiting for her to shut the door and lead the way.

Shannon's movements were slower than she'd like—oh, why hadn't she taken the time for some tea or even coffee this morning?—but she managed to close the door without incident. "Follow me, please."

She started up the stairs and her vision blurred for a moment. Shannon tilted sideways on one of the steps. Pausing, she rubbed the corner of her arid eyes.

"Are you all right?"

If she tried to look back at him, she'd fall for sure. "Mm-hmm." After a deep inhale, she took the steps slowly and finally made it to the top. Steadying herself, Shannon crossed the room —past the couch, past the mantel and bookshelves, past the built-in corner desk—and arrived at the small, circular table next to the tiny kitchen, where she slid into one of the four chairs.

Mr. Peters dawdled along, taking in the home with sweeping glances. The condo may be small, but Shannon hoped that everyone who entered her home felt a sense of calm and peace, which is why she'd chosen to decorate with pastels in a shabby chic style. It made her happy to see the wooden side table she'd found at a garage sale and refinished herself, the walls she'd covered in light floral wallpaper, the knickknacks and photos she'd arranged in a collage on the dining area wall.

But what did Mr. Peters see? Judging by his frown, he wasn't impressed.

"Please, have a seat."

"In a moment." He continued circling her living room, edging closer to her bedroom.

A barrage of barks burst from behind the closed door, each one puncturing Shannon's head.

The social worker leaped back. "You have a dog? He sounds vicious."

"A golden retriever. He's harmless." She shot out of her seat toward her room. "Lucky, no. Stop." The command came out much more high-pitched than she'd intended, but Lucky really was the sweetest dog and rarely barked. Why was he choosing this moment to act like a hound from the depths?

He kept growling and barking, and the veins behind Shannon's eyes throbbed. This was a disaster. She turned to Mr. Peters. "Would you mind if I let him out so he could sniff you and know you're all right? He's really a nice dog, I promise."

"Forgive me if I don't take your word for it." Mr. Peters smoothed a hand over his Friar Tuck–style bald spot.

"I'll be right back then." Shannon slipped into her bedroom, where a four-poster queen bed took up a majority of the space, and squatted down to Lucky's level. "It's okay, boy. Good dog. I'm all right. You can relax."

The dog allowed her to scratch behind his right ear before lying down at the foot of the bed. Shannon returned to the living-slash-dining room to find that Mr. Peters had taken a seat at the table and placed the open file on top. "I'm so sorry about that."

"Seems you've been apologizing a lot lately, Ms. Baker." The man cocked his head. "Are you sure you're ready for this?"

He was talking about the interview ... wasn't he?

Pushing aside the pain in her head, she lowered herself into the chair opposite Mr. Peters. "Yes, I'm ready."

"Very well." The man withdrew a pen from the pocket of his shirt and clicked it. "As you probably know, after this interview, we will determine if you are right for our agency. Then you will be required to take a twelve-week course that focuses largely on self-evaluation and becoming the best foster parent you can be. You'll also have a psychiatric evaluation and, finally, a home inspection."

"Yes, I read up on the process. I've tried to prepare as best I can." She laughed to ease the tension, but it came out garbled.

"Having children is no laughing matter."

What? "Oh, of course—"

"And it's impossible to prepare for completely."

"I know, but—"

"Are you one of those people who feels the need to be in control all the time? Because parenting does not fit neatly into a box. Neither do children."

Was this guy trying to be a jerk? For the first time this morning, Shannon's eyes didn't feel dry. Tears threatened to spill out. But how young and immature would that look? She was twenty-seven, for goodness' sake.

Shannon squared her shoulders, summoning the courage to look Mr. Peters in the eye again. "No, I don't seek control. All of this feels very much outside of my control, actually. I don't know if you saw in my file, but I'm doing this so I can adopt one of my former students. I don't seek control. Just love. I want *him* to feel loved."

And there came the desire to cry again, but this time because of the swelling in her heart.

Yet Mr. Peters appeared unmoved. In fact, his pursed lips and lifted chin and squinty eyes made him look almost … skeptical.

How was this interview going so incredibly wrong? Maybe if

there had been a foster care agency in Walker Beach, with a social worker who knew her—but she'd gone with an agency based in a town thirty minutes away because Noah's social worker had assured her it was the best one, the most efficient at getting through the paperwork.

"Good intentions aside, Ms. Baker, not everyone is fit to be a parent. And that's why I'm here."

Mr. Peters proceeded to ask her about her career, family situation, housing situation, strengths, and weaknesses. It all left her feeling a bit like she was interviewing for a job. Guess she was, really.

But then his questions deepened, prodding her about how she was raised. How was conflict resolved in her home as a child? Did her parents recognize and encourage her skills? How did she get along with her siblings?

And he made up scenarios too, asking her how she'd handle it if she were running late for an important meeting and Noah refused to put on his shoes or get dressed, or what she'd do if a foster child was angry about his birth parents "abandoning" him.

Sure, she had experience dealing with discipline as a preschool teacher, but she hadn't thought through these specific scenarios. And with her lack of sleep, her answers tumbled around in her mind and emerged jumbled and broken—especially when it came to the family of origin questions.

As they neared the end of it all, Shannon's back hurt from sitting so straight, her jaw from clenching it so often. And she only had to view the ever-growing number of creases in Mr. Peters' forehead to realize she was completely bombing this interview.

Finally, he sat back, looked up at her, and closed the file, where he'd taken voracious notes throughout the talk. "There's one more thing I need to address."

"Okay." Already his rapid-fire questions had riddled her with holes, each one hurting more than the last. But what was one more?

"When I first arrived, I could have sworn you were drunk. I need to know if that's something you often do."

"What?" Her jaw dropped and her fingernails bit into her palms as she curled her hands inward. "No, I don't drink. Maybe a glass of wine here or there, but no. I was just really tired. I didn't sleep well last night and had a horrible headache when you arrived."

He whipped the file open again and clicked his pen once more. "Does that happen often? A lack of sleep?" Cocking his head, he waited for her reply.

"Um, sometimes? But no, it's not common."

"Because having children means you probably won't get a lot of sleep. But you still have to be able to function well enough to put their needs first."

"Of course." Shannon blinked past the exhaustion hovering over her.

"And since you don't have a partner to help you, how will you handle those times when you are too tired or too sick to properly care for a child?"

"I don't know. Call my mom probably." Even though her parents had initially been somewhat concerned about her adoption plans, undoubtedly they'd be here if Shannon needed them.

Although they did both work full time. So maybe she should have confirmed their availability before potentially speaking out of turn …

Ugh. She nearly groaned. Quinn would have had a plan outlined and ready to go. She'd have flashed that confident smile and gained Mr. Peters' trust in an instant.

"You don't know?" The man shook his head, closed the file, gathered up his things, and stood. "Maybe you're not as ready as you thought."

Shannon managed a slight nod of her head. A tear splashed onto her hands, finally loosed. Because maybe he was right.

~

Today, Marshall had one job—pick up a pizza for lunch at Tyler and Gabrielle's house.

That's all Quinn trusted him with apparently. Not that he blamed her after last night's fiasco. How had he let himself get so drawn in by a pair of baby blues?

No more. From now on, he was going to stick to Quinn's side like glue, visualize the promotion he had coming, and stay far away from Shannon Baker.

Yeah, the plan hadn't worked so far, but now … well, he just had to remember what was at stake.

Marshall walked down the sidewalk headed for Main Street —specifically, Froggies, the restaurant Quinn's family owned. As he curved around the corner, the church where he'd made a spectacle of himself last night came into view. The ocean glistened just beyond as docked boats bobbed in the marina waters, the sun beating down a happy greeting.

He stopped to admire the view. Man, this place was beautiful —and not baking hot at the moment like Manhattan, where the summer humidity always left him in dire need of a shower after five minutes outside.

And yet, last night he'd been reminded of just how small Walker Beach was. Already today, on his morning run for coffee at the Frosted Cake, he'd been approached by two strangers— Carlotta something and Jim Walsh, the mayor—telling him they'd heard what a great voice he had. Carlotta had waxed on about how amazing it was that he'd gotten "shy Shannon Baker" out of her shell enough to perform. Seemed like she would have talked his ear off completely if Quinn hadn't tugged him away by the elbow.

Much as he'd enjoyed some aspects of being here, he couldn't wait to return to the big city, where his personal life remained his business.

Shaking his head, Marshall took off on his quest for pizza again, but halted at the sight of a blonde with a golden retriever ducking through a small gate next to the church.

Shannon.

And it looked, by all accounts, like she was crying as she disappeared from his view.

Aw, man. Marshall lifted his hands to the back of his head, threading his fingers together as he looked upward. What did he do now? He'd been so determined to stay focused—but she was alone except for her dog, and something was clearly wrong.

Before he could change his mind, he followed her. On the other side of the gate, the vista opened up completely, unblocked by buildings or boardwalks. A bed of grass covered the church's backyard and abutted the sand of the public beach. And there sat Shannon on the edge of the grass, her face buried in Lucky's fur, shoulders heaving.

His heart tugged him forward. "Hey."

She started and glanced up, streaks of black running down her cheeks. "Marshall? What are you doing here?"

"I saw you slip back this way." He paused. "Are you okay?"

"No. No, I'm not." Then tears came again and she pulled her knees to her chest and dropped her face into her palms.

Okay, that was it. Marshall sat next to her, draping his arm around her shoulders. "Whatever it is, it'll be all right."

"N-no, it w-won't." Her breaths shuddered in and out. "I f-failed him."

"Failed who?"

"N-Noah." Then she turned and buried her face in Marshall's chest. He wrapped his arms fully around her and let her cry, running his hands lightly down her back in the soothing way his mom used to do when he was sick. Marshall stroked her hair and—oh man—it was softer than he'd even imagined.

Stop thinking about how good this feels and stay focused on her, you idiot.

When she'd finally calmed a bit, he couldn't help but place the whisper of a kiss against her hair. "Wanna talk about it?"

At first, she remained silent. But then, the whole story spilled from her. The interview. The way the social worker had despised her from the beginning. *The moron.* The family of origin questions that had rocked her. "I mean, it's like he knew exactly what to ask to tear open my heart."

Marshall didn't pry. If she wanted to tell him more, she would.

Shannon pulled back, her eyes swollen, nose red. "I'm so sorry. I didn't mean to ..."

But he tightened his grip around her, keeping her firmly entrenched in his embrace. "Don't be sorry. I'm sorry you had to go through that alone." Stupid Mr. Peters, making Shannon feel bad for being single and wanting to foster a child. He'd better hope Marshall never got a few minutes alone with him. "Maybe you could call his superior and complain about his unprofessionalism."

"Oh no, I'm sure it was my fault. I was tired and not thinking straight." Gently, she scooted a few inches away from Marshall's arms and back toward her dog, who lay on her other side. Shannon stared out at the horizon. "His job is to make sure foster kids are placed in good homes, with parents who have their own lives together enough to take care of someone else. And even though I want that more than anything, maybe ..."

"Hey, look at me."

A tick flickered on her jaw, but after a few beats, she did.

"Don't let his lies infect you. You will be an amazing mother, and anyone who says otherwise doesn't know what they're talking about."

Her lips crinkled at the edges, like she didn't believe him. "You're sweet."

"I'm serious. The thing you want more than anything in the world is to give Noah a home. That's an amazing dream, and it is proof of how incredible you are."

She certainly had *him* beat. Marshall's biggest dream in life was a promotion. A promotion that, apparently, meant so much that he'd been willing to lie to this beautiful woman in front of him.

And he couldn't do it anymore.

"Shannon ..." Marshall touched her hand.

But she slipped it out of his reach. "Thank you for the shoulder to cry on and the sweet words, Marshall. But I should be going." Snagging Lucky's leash, Shannon stood.

"Wait." Scrambling up, Marshall found himself toe to toe with her. He reached out and held fast to the leash. "I need to tell you something."

"I can't, Marshall. This ..." Shannon shook her head. "I appreciate your friendship, I really do, but ..."

She probably considered him a cad. Well, he might be, but not for the reasons she thought. "Shannon, I know you're probably going to hate me when I say this, but—"

"Then don't say it ... because I don't want to hate you."

No way she'd ever forgive him after this, but he had to tell her the truth. *Just blurt it out.* "I'm not really Quinn's boyfriend."

She dropped Lucky's leash. "What?" Her eyes belied her confusion.

"I'm just a coworker she convinced at the last minute to come here and pretend to be in a relationship with her." The words tumbled from his lips faster than a ten-car pileup.

Turning, Shannon ran both of her hands over her forehead and through her hair. "But why would she ...?"

If the woman would only look at him ... "Her real boyfriend

dumped her on Friday. I don't know why she didn't just come clean to you all about it."

"So you're not together? You don't love my sister?"

"No. And no. I'm completely single."

Finally she looked at him again. Opened her mouth as if to say something, then snapped it shut. Red rose in her cheeks and her gaze fled to the ground. "I don't know what to say."

Praying it wasn't the wrong thing to do, he gently turned her back toward him and nudged her chin upward with his index finger. Hurt swirled in the depths of her eyes.

"You don't have to say anything. I just wanted you to know."

Marshall's hand fell as Shannon stepped away from him. She grabbed Lucky's leash once more and took off at a clipped pace through the grass and out the gate.

He'd probably just shot himself in the foot regarding his promotion. She was going to tell everyone. But he couldn't blame her. He only had himself to blame.

For the lies, yes. But also for the aching emptiness of his arms.

Because he'd gone and done the one thing he'd promised himself he'd never do again—Marshall St. John had started to care about someone who had the ability to hurt him.

CHAPTER 6

"*I'm not really Quinn's boyfriend.*"

The words beat a path around and around Shannon's brain as she hurried up Main Street, Lucky in tow. Marshall had lied to her. He was a liar.

He was also single.

Groaning, she tugged Lucky's leash as the dog stopped to smell a pot of flowers outside Hardings Market. "No, boy."

Man, what a confusing day. First the interview, then Marshall. If Shannon had her way, she'd go straight home, curl up to watch a romance flick, and try to forget this awful day had ever happened. But first, she had to do her Baker family reunion duty and check in with her cousin Cameron about tomorrow night's event.

After a few minutes of walking, she came upon Rise Beach Rentals, which Cam managed for an older couple who lived out of town. The pale green storefront had a small porch with a white railing and a large colorful sign out front, designating it as the place to get all manner of beach supplies—from kayaks to bikes to jet skis.

Shannon tied Lucky to a cute black lamppost and walked

inside. Two kayaks were mounted to one wall along with a colorful display of paddles painted different bright colors. A few young tourists browsed a catalog of available supplies, and a woman in a wet suit filled out a form at the front desk, where Jenna Wakefield stood playing with a paperclip.

Their eyes connected and a wide smile stretched across Jenna's face. "Shannon! Hey!"

"Hi." Her voice still wobbled despite her best efforts.

The browsing customers briefly flicked their gazes toward Shannon before going back to their own business, and the one with the paperwork finished and slid it toward Jenna.

Jenna held up a finger to Shannon. "Be right with you, okay?"

"No problem." She was here to talk to Cameron anyway, though there was a chance he was giving a kayak tour or snagging lunch or doing a million other things. Either way, she just needed to confirm he had everything handled for tomorrow and then she could bury herself in blankets at home.

Maybe she'd even get the courage to text her parents and beg off of the Marvel-themed trivia tonight. Because the thought of facing Marshall and Quinn after everything she'd learned today …

Jenna finally finished ringing up her customer and disappeared into the back, re-emerging with a beach umbrella and snorkeling equipment for two. Somehow she handled the bulk like a pro without fumbling. Did becoming a mother make a woman more nimble? Shannon had seen countless young moms around town carting kids, strollers, and bags like pack mules, so it was possible.

Noah wasn't a baby, but maybe Shannon would—

The truth smacked her in the gut again. That dream might be gone, all because she'd taken her eye off the prize and allowed herself to be distracted.

By a liar.

She faced the wall and squeezed her eyes shut, but more tears wouldn't come. Seems she'd loosed them all on Marshall's shirt.

"Sorry about that." Jenna's voice popped up behind her.

Shannon turned toward her sort-of-friend-sort-of-family-member. A quick scan showed they were alone in the store. "No problem." Her voice scraped the air.

"Whoa, you okay?" Shannon attempted a nod, but Jenna frowned. "What's wrong?"

"Nothing."

Cocking her head, Jenna placed her hands firmly on her waist. "Shannon Baker, I've never seen you look more pitiful. Has Quinn been saying mean things again?"

"Again?"

Her hands waved in the air. "Yes, again. I know we weren't close in high school, but I saw the way she treated everyone, including you." She lowered her voice and leaned closer—as if there were anyone else to hear her. "And I remember the whole Cody Briggs thing too."

Shannon's cheeks were suddenly warm as she approached the front desk. "It isn't Quinn this time." Not directly anyway. She blew out a breath. "I think I bombed my foster care interview this morning."

"What? You? No way. You're more qualified than me to be a mom." Jenna joined her at the desk and leaned sideways against it, facing Shannon.

A staccato laugh left Shannon's throat. "That's hardly true."

"Please, girl. I was seventeen when I had Liam. And I've been a depressed mess for most of his life."

Gabrielle never spoke ill of Jenna, but she had confided in Shannon a year ago about her sister's struggles with mental health. Since then, Jenna had blossomed before the town's eyes, becoming healthier, stronger, and more outwardly joyful, but who knew what demons she still fought on the inside.

Shannon reached out to squeeze Jenna's arm. "You are an amazing mom because you love your son and would do anything for him."

Something flashed in Jenna's eyes, but it was gone quickly, replaced with a softening. "Anyone who has seen you with Noah knows he holds a special place in your heart. Now, give me this idiot social worker's number and I'll pound him into dust for you."

That made Shannon laugh—the idea of wispy Jenna Wakefield beating anyone up. "Thanks, but I'm afraid only divine intervention will work at this point. I failed really badly, Jenna."

"I'm sure it's not as bad as you think." Jenna chewed her thumbnail as she studied Shannon. "And I don't want to discourage you by any means, but … just make sure being a mom is what you really want. It's hard to be single, to be raising Liam alone, and for years I had the blessing of Gabrielle living with us and doing more for me than any sister should have to do. Now that I'm finally standing on my own two feet—barely, it feels like sometimes—it's really difficult. And while motherhood is the biggest blessing of my life, I don't know that I would have chosen to do it alone."

"Thank you for telling me that." It probably hadn't been easy to admit. "But nothing is more important to me than Noah finding a happy home."

Oh man, guess she did have some tears left. One trickled down her cheek and she swiped at it. "Anyway, I didn't come here to dump all of that on you. I came to see Cam."

At the mention of her boss, who was also a friend, Jenna's eyes betrayed something else altogether—maybe a spark of interest, one Shannon had suspected for some time.

"He's in back. Let me get him for you." With quick steps, Jenna headed through the wide door behind the desk. A minute later, she came back, her manager in tow.

Cam's face lit up with an easy smile. "If you're here to check on tomorrow night, I've got it all handled, little cuz."

Shannon grinned at the moniker, though she supposed he did have nearly a decade on her. "I tried texting you, but didn't hear back, so just wanted to be sure you didn't need my help with any of it." A month ago, Cam had volunteered to organize the beach games part of the event, while Mom had gladly offered to head up the chili-salsa competition.

Jenna snickered. "We all know how good Cam is about returning texts or phone calls."

Cameron whistled a line of "Everything's Gonna Be Alright." "I just live life, man. Don't want to be weighed down by technology."

"If only we all could have such luxuries," Jenna teased.

"You could join me." He poked her in the side.

Her eyes lit up as she struggled to hold back a smile. "Someone has to be responsible around here."

Shannon followed their volley of teasing, wondering if they'd notice if she slipped out. There was definitely something between them, even if Cameron seemed oblivious to the way Jenna looked at him.

Her cousin laughed at Jenna's reply and turned to Shannon. "Oh hey, your performance with Marshall last night … wow, cuz, I didn't know you had it in you."

Wonderful. Did her entire family think her a boyfriend stealer? "Um …"

Jenna's eyebrows shot up. "Performance?"

"Yeah, Shannon was amazing. She and Quinn's latest boy toy from New York sang this duet, and man. I didn't know you had pipes on you like that."

The tightening in her chest lessened. "It was nothing. Just a bit of fun."

Keep telling yourself that.

Cameron checked his watch. "Oh, I've gotta go prep for our

afternoon surf lesson. I'll see you tonight, Shan. And don't worry about tomorrow. I've got it handled." After giving her a quick hug in his big arms, he left.

"I'll see you later, Jenna." Shannon tucked her hands into the back pockets of her jean shorts. "Thanks for earlier."

"Wait just a minute. This performance with Marshall— what's that all about?"

The woman was way too perceptive. Shannon fiddled with a jar of paperclips on the desktop. "He just asked me to sing with him and I couldn't ..."

"Say no?"

Shannon's gaze collided with Jenna's face, which wore a knowing expression. "It's not like that. He's just ..."

"A friend?"

Snagging a paperclip from the jar, Shannon worked it into a straight line. "Yes. No." Oh, she was going to burst if she didn't tell someone. And she couldn't tell Ashley, her normal go-to confidante who was busy with Ben and Bella's wedding ... and her new husband. The thought still stung.

And besides, Jenna was outside the family drama but close enough to understand it. Maybe she was the perfect person to tell. "You have to keep this between us, all right?"

"My lips are sealed." Jenna's fingers zipped across her mouth.

"Yes, I may have developed a bit of a ... crush. I actually met Marshall before I knew he was Quinn's boyfriend." She told Jenna about that day on the beach.

Crossing her arms, she frowned. "Sounds like he was flirting with you while dating another woman."

"It looked like that, but ..." Here went nothing. "I found out that they're just pretending to date."

"What? Why?"

"Quinn's boyfriend broke up with her. I'm not sure why Marshall agreed to help, though." She hadn't stuck around long enough to ask. "But the fact he lied ... that means I should stay far, far away from him, right?" Shannon took another paper clip out and unwrapped it, one metal end digging into her fingertips.

"Generally I'd say yes. I've dealt with my fair share of liars." Jenna tapped her chin. "But I also know your sister. She could convince a starving man to give her his last bite of bread."

That was the truest thing anyone had said to Shannon all day. All week. All year.

"So if Marshall means something to you, if you think there could be more between you, then ask him for the truth. All of it. And then decide what to do."

Marshall should have gotten on a plane back to New York as soon as he'd told Shannon the truth. And yet here he stood, hand in hand with Quinn. They walked with Tyler and Gabrielle back to their house after Trivia Night, the cool night breeze rustling the collar of Marshall's shirt.

"I still can't believe we won." Quinn let loose a girly *woo-hoo* across Main Street. "You did me proud, little brother."

At least someone was happy. For Marshall, it had been a miserable night—all the pretending, all the lies. And Shannon hadn't even been there, so he was left to wonder what she was thinking about his revelation earlier in the day.

Yep, miserable.

"Why can't you believe it? I know everything there is to know about Marvel." Even with his arm wrapped around Gabrielle's shoulders, Tyler managed to puff out his chest.

His wife laughed. "He really does. Me? I'll take *Pride & Prejudice* any day. But what do you think he wants to watch every Friday night?"

"That's how you spend a Friday night?" The light from the streetlamp caught the flicker off Quinn's dangling gold earrings as she shook her head. "You old married people are so boring."

"Someday you'll understand." A secret smile slid across Gabrielle's lips. Meanwhile, her hand seemed permanently attached to her stomach, stroking it.

Marshall had always been in the same camp as Quinn. He loved nothing more than heading to the bar at ten p.m. on Friday, working off the stress of another long week with a beer in one hand and a microphone in the other.

Back at his apartment, it was too quiet. His three roommates were never there, and even when the TV was blaring, a sense of quiet forever pervaded the place.

But what if someone *were* there at the end of a long day? Someone who could help him shoulder his burdens. Who'd curl up with him on the couch and nerd out over the movies he liked —or at least tolerate them with a smile.

Who'd remind him he wasn't alone like he'd been ever since Mom died eleven years ago.

Shannon's face popped into his mind, and suddenly, the idea wasn't half as bad as it had always seemed.

"Ow." Quinn pulled her hand away from Marshall's and massaged it with the other. "Honey, you squeezed too hard."

He had? "Sorry." Not really. It gave him an excuse to sink his hands into his pockets.

"Is there something you wanted to say?"

"No, just admiring the view." They stepped off Main Street and into Tyler and Gabrielle's neighborhood. A brick house that was one step shy of being a mansion towered over them. Sprinklers tossed water across its pristine lawn.

Quinn laughed. "It's just plain old Walker Beach. Not terribly exciting." She elbowed Tyler. "I'm still surprised you came back and settled here. Don't you miss the nightlife, the verve of Manhattan?"

"Sure, sometimes." The former football player shrugged his

shoulders. "But I get back there often enough for meetings. And this is where our family is."

"Exactly."

"Someday you're going to miss it too, Quinnie."

"I highly doubt that, Ty Ty."

Marshall listened to the siblings tease each other and glanced up at the sky, where a thousand different stars sent light tumbling through space to reach them here, like the coolest magic trick ever invented. Definitely couldn't see that in the city.

Gabrielle leaned forward as she walked, fixing her gaze on Quinn. "Soon you'll have a good enough reason to come visit, though. Your new niece will probably have you wrapped around her little finger."

Huffing, Quinn's steps faltered a bit, but she righted herself quickly as they rounded the corner to Tyler and Gabrielle's house. "I think you're confusing me with Shannon. She's the one who's good with kids."

The house came into view in front of them, and Quinn threw open the gate on the white picket fence. "I have a headache. I'm going to bed." Then she strode toward the house.

Gabrielle turned worried eyes on Tyler. "I'm really trying. I just don't think she likes me."

"It's not personal, Gabs. She has a headache. You remember how cranky she gets when she doesn't feel well." Tyler kissed Gabrielle's forehead, then turned to Marshall. "Want to join me in the back? I've got a little project for us."

Marshall should probably check on his work email, but it could wait a bit. "Sure."

After hugging his wife, Tyler led the way around the side of the house into the back, where a modest patch of grass extended to a brick-walled fence surrounding the yard. Then he rounded on Marshall.

"Do you love my sister?"

Whoa. The guy was cutting right to the chase. Marshall could admire that. He just wasn't quite sure what he was supposed to say.

But Tyler didn't give him a chance to answer. "Because the way you look at her isn't how a man in love usually looks. You almost seem ... I don't know, pained or something." The guy frowned. "And it's totally different from the way you look at Shannon."

Spots crowded the edges of Marshall's vision. "What? That's ... crazy." He nearly groaned at the weakness in his own voice. But he couldn't help the fact he'd always been a terrible liar, even as a kid.

And until now, he hadn't had to do much direct lying, just mostly going along with what Quinn said. But they hadn't fooled Quinn's twin. Just how much did he suspect?

Marshall sighed. "Look, man ..." But what could he say? Even Marshall didn't understand why Quinn was doing this, other than embarrassment over being dumped just before the reunion.

Silent, maybe even brooding, Tyler walked a little way into the yard, and Marshall followed him. This small corner of the yard held a raised flower bed, where some purple flowers Marshall didn't recognize grew, their buds just starting to open. A few other holes had been dug but remained empty despite the gold flowers sitting next to the bed in temporary black pots. Someone obviously had unfinished business here.

Tyler looked Marshall square in the eye. "My sisters are complicated. Quinn puts on this tough act, but ..." His jaw flexed. "And Shannon. She's fragile, especially when it comes to Quinn. There's history there you don't know about."

How should Marshall respond? He wanted to defend Shannon. She was delicate, yes, and sensitive, but he got the feeling she was a lot stronger than anyone gave her credit for—herself included.

But the curiosity to understand the sisterly dynamics took precedence. "So tell me."

"I shouldn't." Tyler kicked at a clump of dirt, which broke open to reveal a mess of tiny roots. Lowering himself to his knees in front of the flower bed, he slipped on a worn pair of gardening gloves that looked a bit too small.

Huh. Marshall hadn't figured Tyler for the gardening type. Or maybe it was normally Gabrielle's job but she couldn't do it right now.

The things a man in love did. Marshall's heart rate escalated at the thought.

Tyler snatched up a nearby hand trowel and handed it to Marshall, who took it. "As you can probably tell, my sisters are complete opposites. Always have been. But there was a time when we all got along—as well as most siblings, anyway."

Marshall squatted.

"We need about eight holes." Tyler pointed from the bed to the unplanted flowers.

"Got it."

"Not too deep though. Maybe about six inches." Tyler took hold of the first plant and shook the plastic pot loose, revealing a half-foot of packed dirt in a rounded square shape at the bottom. "Anyway, Quinn and my mom were in this car accident when we were kids, and a lot of things changed then. I'm sure she's told you all about that though."

No, but Marshall couldn't exactly admit that to Tyler. He dug the trowel into the soft soil, the wooden handle rough against his palm.

"But what she maybe hasn't told you about is this guy in high school. Cody something. I don't know all the details, but suffice it to say that Shannon liked him—but Quinn got him."

With a much-too-vigorous plunge into the dirt, the tip of Marshall's trowel flew up, flinging soil backward into his face. He coughed and spit the dirt out of his mouth.

"Dude, you okay? I know it's no fun to think about your girl with another guy, but it was a long time ago."

Sure, let him think that. "I'm fine."

"The good news is she dumped him when she left for college in New York." After placing his flowers in one of the previously dug holes, Tyler pulled in the dirt around it, smoothing and patting until the flower looked like it had been there all along. "They were only together for a few months."

Sounded like the poor sap had escaped Quinn's clutches. Marshall grunted, and for a while, the guys worked in silence, Marshall digging while Tyler planted.

Finally they finished, a complete flower bed now assembled. Tyler tugged off the gloves and wiped his brow with his forearm. "Gabrielle is going to be happy when she wakes up and sees this tomorrow. Thanks, man."

"No problem." And because he was a glutton for punishment, Marshall cocked his head and narrowed his eyes slightly at Tyler, trying to figure the guy out. "Much as I like the idea of making a pregnant woman smile, I'm guessing you had a point in bringing me out here?"

Tyler hesitated before nodding. "I know you're not a bad dude, Marshall. But you need to be careful with my sisters' hearts. The last guy that came between them, well … I think it broke something in both of them. It definitely drove a wedge. And I don't want that to happen again."

If only Tyler knew the truth. But if Marshall told him, there was no way he'd keep it to himself. The whole family would know, and then whatever secrets Quinn was trying to keep would be exposed.

And yeah, Marshall wasn't so selfless as to forget the impact it would have on his life too. His future. But he really did hate the idea of Tyler thinking badly of him, especially since Marshall still managed Amazing Kids Foundation's account at the firm. But also, because Quinn and Shannon's brother was a good guy, and Marshall respected him.

"Tyler ..."

"All I'm saying is, it'd be better for you to leave and not look back than to continue down the path you're on."

Marshall couldn't argue with him there. And if he were a stronger man, he would listen.

But the idea of never seeing Shannon again, of never having the chance to explain himself further ...

Just call him a weakling, because his emotional muscles had the strength of an infant.

CHAPTER 7

"*So* *if Marshall means something to you, if you think there could be more between you, then ask him for the truth. All of it. And then decide what to do.*"

Shannon couldn't get Jenna's words out of her brain—nor the fact that she was about to have ample opportunity to find out the truth if she wanted to.

But did she? Wasn't it better to let Marshall go? After all, he was still here in town, pretending to be Quinn's boyfriend a day after he'd told Shannon the truth. He must assume she wasn't going to tell anyone, figured he could continue getting away with it so he could ... what?

Why was he doing this?

"Argh." She pounded her fist against the arm of her couch. Lucky's head popped up from his place on the rug in front of the entertainment center.

Shannon sighed. "Sorry, boy. I'm just frustrated."

The doorbell rang. Lucky barked and looked at her.

"And scared. I'm scared, Luck." She stayed frozen to her spot, no internal pep talks working to get her up and to the door.

When it rang again a minute later, Lucky jumped to his feet and ran down the stairs.

You can do this. It's just a final planning session.

Right. She didn't have to ask Marshall anything she didn't want to. They'd keep it strictly business.

Shannon heaved herself to her feet and trudged down the stairs. Nudging Lucky aside, she smoothed her shirt and opened the door.

Marshall stood there with a bouquet of purple daisies. "Hey, Shannon."

How did the man look so achingly handsome in khaki shorts, brown leather sandals, and a red polo shirt?

Strictly business. Yeah, right.

"Hi." Shannon tucked a loose piece of hair behind her ear, then stepped aside. "Come on in."

"These are for you."

"Thank you." She took the flowers he extended and couldn't help lifting them to her nose, inhaling the sweet scent.

"I know we need to review everything for the picnic tomorrow night, but do you think we could talk first?"

No. "Okay." After shutting the door, she led him up the stairs, Lucky at her heels.

At the top of the steps, Marshall allowed his gaze to roam the living room. "Wow, your place is great." He absently patted the dog's head. "It's so ... you."

"Thanks." Trying to ignore the swelling of her chest at the compliment, Shannon laid the flowers on the kitchen counter. "What did you want to talk about?"

"Yesterday. Everything. I need to explain."

Nodding, she glanced up into his chocolate eyes. Nope, she couldn't have this conversation. Not face-to-face anyway. "Would you like to help me make salsa for the competition tonight while we talk?"

"Sure. Put me to work."

Flitting about the kitchen, she gathered the vegetables they'd need then placed a wooden cutting board, knife, and red onion in front of him. "Chop about a fourth of this."

"Will do."

As Marshall washed and dried his hands, Shannon set herself up with some tomatoes. They both started chopping, the *thwack* of the knives against wood falling into a steady rhythm.

"I want to apologize again for lying to you."

She just barely missed nicking one of her fingers with her thin knife. "It's okay."

"Shannon, if someone lies to you, it's not okay." *Thwack, thwack, thwack.*

"You're right. It's not okay." Tomato juice squirted across the board. "So, why did you do it?"

Silence filled the space between them.

Finally ... "I don't want you to think less of me when I tell you."

Why did he care what *she* thought? Heat flushed through her. "I'll try to keep an open mind."

"Quinn promised she'd recommend me for an upper management position at work."

"You're lying to get a promotion?" That didn't sound like the Marshall she'd come to know. Maybe she'd only fooled herself into thinking the guy she'd met on the beach last weekend was really a prince.

"It sounds really bad when you put it like that."

"Sorry." Picking up the cutting board with one hand, she used the knife to scrape the tomatoes into a glass bowl. Then Shannon snagged the green onions she'd bought. "What about your job do you love so much that you're willing to go to such great lengths?"

"Are you kidding? I don't even *like* my job half the time." He paused. "Hey, I'm done. Where do you want these?"

"Over here." With the knife, she pointed to the bowl of tomatoes.

Marshall poured the result of his labor into the bowl. The scent of freshly cut onion filled Shannon's nose. "You have more for me to do?"

Evaluating what she had left to chop, she handed the green onions off to him. "Do two of these, please." Then she took the jalapeño off the counter and washed it. "So if you don't like your job, why do you work there?"

"I'm good at it. And I'm building up a nest egg." He shrugged then went back to the cutting board. "Right now I make beans compared to upper management."

She cut the seeds from the jalapeño core. "Sure, it's nice to have money. But what about doing something you love? Something that makes you happy?"

"Most people don't get that luxury. Besides, life isn't about happiness. It's about finding purpose. And one way you find that is to set goals." Marshall grunted. "My dad used to say that when you reach one goal, you set another and another. You never stop climbing, never stop reaching for success—whatever that means to you. And even though I don't have one iota of respect left for the man, I think he has a point. To get anywhere in life, you need to have a goal."

She stopped chopping and turned to look at him. Why didn't he respect his dad? Shannon wanted to ask, but the moment didn't feel right. Still, his views on life—and work—made her long to give him a hug.

Well, she couldn't do *that*.

He looked up, met her gaze. "You got really quiet. What are you thinking?"

"That just seems like a really hard way to live. Like you could never be content or satisfied with what you have."

"I can see what you mean, but it's better than sitting around being complacent, isn't it? Better than letting life pass you by without fighting for what you want?"

Something in his comment tapped at a corner of her heart, asking it to open. Shannon frowned. "And what you want is this promotion? *That's* what gives your life purpose?" And was he equating purpose with meaning? What a sad thing, for a job to define him—especially when she could somehow see, despite the lies, that he was so much *more*.

"Marshall, first of all, if you are as hard a worker as you say you are, then I don't think you really need my sister to recommend you." Into the bowl went the jalapeño. "And second, you are more than what you do. You know that, right?"

Shannon washed her hands and started toward the cupboard to gather the spices she'd need to complete the salsa, but Marshall stepped in front of her, his fingers lightly grasping her elbow. "Shannon, thank you. I ..."

The air around them grew static, full of something charged. He wrapped his hand fully around her waist, gently tugging her toward him till she finally took a step closer. Her hands found a home on his chest and she fiddled with one of the little white buttons on his shirt.

His Adam's apple bobbed as Marshall swallowed, his gaze flicking briefly to her lips. As he leaned down, she smelled the mint on his breath.

Her heart hammered. Oh, how she ached to finally be kissed. How she ached to be kissed by *Marshall*.

But Shannon held up her hand to his lips, effectively stopping him from moving closer. Because she still couldn't trust him, right? Besides, what good would it do to allow herself to be pulled in by him? It's not like they could have a relationship. The whole town thought he was with her sister, for goodness' sake.

Not to mention the fact he cared about his job so much he was willing to lie for it, which meant he'd never stay in Walker

Beach long term. And, even if she'd bombed her foster care interview and lost her chance at being Noah's mom, Shannon would never leave the boy alone in Walker Beach. Much as she hated to admit it, there was no future with Marshall St. John.

No scenario in which she gave him her heart and he didn't break it.

"Shannon. Look at me."

But she couldn't, or she'd be a goner. Glancing away, Shannon spotted the daisies on the counter next to them. The perfect excuse. "Oh, I totally forgot that I need to put those flowers in water."

In two steps, she was out of his embrace and standing by her kitchen sink, rustling in the cabinet underneath. Once she had a medium-sized glass vase in hand, she began to fill it with water.

"You want to know why I got you daisies?"

"Because they were the cheapest flower in the store?" Flecks of water wet her fingertips.

"No." He chuckled, coming within reach again, leaning against the counter nearby.

She peeked up at him. The intensity rolling off his gaze made her feel like M&Ms in the palm of a hand. Did he know what he was doing to her? How could she possibly maintain her distance with him looking so delicious, being so incredibly sweet?

"It's because daisies are not roses. They're not lilies or whatever fancy flowers people buy for an anniversary or a first date or to tell their significant other that they're special. Daisies are like the underdogs of the floral world."

Stomach fluttering, she shut off the water and placed the vase on the counter before unwrapping the flowers from the crinkling cellophane. Shannon took the flowers out one by one, assessing where they should go to create the most beautiful bouquet possible.

"But, according to the nice man at the flower shop—"

"Lee Rivas?"

"Yes, him. According to Lee, daisies have a lot of hidden powers, like their medicinal properties." Marshall picked up a daisy from the cellophane, turning it over and examining it from every angle. "Apparently they're known as the gardener's friend because they can ease an aching back."

"Okay…" Where was he going with this?

Marshall plopped the final daisy into the vase. It's not where she would have placed it, but nestled in among its friends, it still looked beautiful.

And, oh goodness, now he was only a hairsbreadth away. Goosebumps slid down the curve of her neck.

"Daisies also symbolize purity, beauty, loyal love, and patience. Shannon, they remind me of you." Leaning toward her, Marshall's lips brushed the tip of her ear as he lowered his voice, husky yet strong. "You ease the aches of everyone around you, your beauty is pure, and you are loyal in your love and patient with those of us who don't deserve it."

She closed her eyes, savoring his words, his nearness.

"And you, Shannon Baker, just like these daisies, are severely underrated."

CHAPTER 8

*T*oday was supposed to be a happy day. A day to celebrate love.

So why this heaviness in Shannon's limbs as she waited outside her Aunt Lisa and Uncle Frank's house, staring at the pink and silver balloons attached to the mailbox?

A few leaves from the tree overhead dropped and swirled at Shannon's feet. This was ridiculous. She was one of Bella's bridesmaids and this was her friend's bridal shower. And even though she'd spent last night here decorating instead of playing games at the cookout—which she'd skipped—she should have been by a half-hour ago to help with last-minute prep.

Instead, she'd stayed in bed extra long, staring at the ceiling fan blades turning, turning, replaying the scene in her kitchen yesterday. Wondering if she should have just kissed Marshall and asked questions later.

But he hadn't indicated that he and Quinn would be giving up their charade. And that was a problem.

Then again, she hadn't asked him to. How would he have responded to such a request?

"Shannon!"

Gripping the handle of the purple gift bag in her hands, Shannon startled at the voice coming from the doorway.

Fresh and glowing in a pair of white linen pants and a bright green off-the-shoulder blouse, Shannon's cousin Ashley closed the door behind her and headed down the brick path to the mailbox. She leaned in for a quick hug. "Everything okay? You were just standing here."

"Me? Oh yeah, fine. Just … tired."

"With good reason. You've been handling so much with the reunion, and I can't thank you enough." Ashley smoothed back a piece of her hair, the princess-cut diamond on her ring finger a glaring reminder of her love story.

Shannon looked away. "It's been no problem."

"Hey." Ashley touched her shoulder. "You sure it's just tiredness? I've been meaning to ask about the adoption process. Don't you have an interview this week?"

Any other time and Ashley would have been the one to know all the details first. But not only had her cousin been surrounded at pretty much every reunion event—family members clamoring to hear how she and Derek had gotten together—but she'd also chosen to get married without Shannon there.

Maybe she meant more to Shannon than Shannon did to her.

And Shannon wasn't bitter. She wasn't. She just felt … sad. Okay, and maybe a little betrayed. But today was about honoring Bella.

Straightening her shoulders, Shannon forced a smile and linked arms with Ashley. They started to walk toward the door. "The interview was on Tuesday. It went terribly."

Ashley stilled. "What happened? Are you okay?"

"No." Despite her efforts, Shannon's mutinous chin trembled. "But I'm doing my best to keep going this week. There's just been a lot to deal with."

"Shannon." Ashley tucked her arms fully around Shannon, cocooning her into the familiar bond they'd always had—cousins, but more like sisters really. "I'm sorry. I didn't know. I've been so caught up with finishing Ben and Bella's wedding prep ..."

And eloping. An ice pick stabbed Shannon's heart. She pulled away from her cousin, swiping her eyes. "It's fine. Really. I don't want you to worry about it. I'm sure it'll all work out."

A few guests arrived—Heather and Christina Campbell, Ashley's new sisters-in-law—and after greeting them with hugs and promises to catch up inside, Ashley pulled Shannon off the walkway and under the shade of a huge California oak tree that stood taller than the two-story house.

"I know how much you want to adopt Noah." Ashley chewed her bottom lip. "But maybe this is a sign, you know? Maybe you're just supposed to be his teacher, a friend, a mentor—not his mom."

Despite Ashley's attempt at encouragement, her words left Shannon feeling like she stood too close to a fire, hot embers flying out to land on her skin.

"I don't *want* to be just a teacher or friend or mentor." Shannon's hand flew to her heart, thumped it twice. "I want to be his mom. Don't you think I can do it?"

Her cousin's eyes widened. "Of course I do. I've already told you that. I just wonder if you've set your heart on this path and forgotten that you can still have an impact on Noah's life in other ways. A huge impact."

Chest tightening, Shannon's blood raced in her veins and she was very near weeping right here in her aunt's front yard. "We should get inside." And before Ashley could respond, she strode toward the front door, her skirt swishing at her knees.

As she entered the house, laughter and chatter filled her ears. Shannon moved through the front hallway into the massive living room, where at least forty women roamed, eating tiny quiches, fruit, and all manner of pastries. Josephine Radcliffe stood behind the white marble breakfast bar, helping Shannon's much older cousin Elise Griffin—Cameron and the other sextuplets' mom—load up platters of food. Meanwhile, her aunts Jules and Kiki replenished the punch bowl with pink juice and plops of sherbet.

Bella stood near the white fireplace chatting with her maid of honor, Jessica—who lived in Los Angeles—Jenna, and librarian Madison Price. The bride-to-be glanced up at Shannon's and Ashley's approach. "There are the rest of my bridesmaids! Let's get this party started." The woman's strong arms squeezed the breath out of Shannon as they hugged. "But first, Madison was just about to tell us some news."

"What news?" Dressed in dark skinny jeans, a crisp white button-up, and red pumps, Quinn joined the small grouping, a plate of goodies in her hand.

Guess she couldn't avoid her sister forever. Shannon glanced away.

All eyes turned back to Madison, who held up her left hand. "Evan proposed last night."

Squeals filled the air, questions flying about how he'd done it. Ashley stood there quiet and grinning. She and Madison had been close since Madison's return to Walker Beach in January, so it wasn't surprising that Madison would have told her before everyone else.

They must be better friends than Ashley and Shannon, since *Madison* had been invited to Ashley's wedding-slash-elopement.

Ugh. Shannon tried her best to stuff the green monster back into the cage of her heart as Madison told the story of how Evan had taken her for a picnic at Walker Beach Park, and, on the pitcher's mound of the baseball fields where they'd had their first date, told her he'd been waiting for the right pitch and, now, with her, he was ready to run the bases of life if she'd have him.

The women all oohed and aahed, and Shannon's eyes drifted upward, pain radiating in her jaw from clenching it too tightly. Over the wooden mantel hung a hand-painted sign that read Be Still My Soul.

Be still. Yes. Shannon blew out a breath.

What was the matter with her? She was happy for all of her family and friends who had found love. Really she was. But was it too much to hope that maybe—someday—she'd find someone to love her?

"Daisies also symbolize purity, beauty, loyal love, and patience. Shannon, they remind me of you."

Shannon pinched her elbows to bring herself back to reality.

"What about you, Quinn?" Bella turned to Shannon's sister, who was just popping a blueberry between her teeth. "Are you and Marshall pretty serious? Any proposals in your future?"

Quinn chewed, her gaze thoughtful, then swallowed. "I sure hope so."

Catching Jenna's raised eyebrows aimed her direction, Shannon rolled her eyes.

Her sister's gaze shot to hers, narrowed. "He's very much in love with me. Told me so last night."

What a load of crock. The tips of Shannon's ears burned. She coughed. "Excuse me. I need some punch." Backing away, she headed for the drink station.

Before she reached it, a hand gripped her elbow. "We need to talk," her sister's voice hissed in her ear.

Quinn practically dragged Shannon down the hallway toward an empty guest room. Lavender permeated the air but did nothing to calm the quivering in Shannon's stomach, nor the tightness in Quinn's features.

Her sister closed the door and whirled around. "What was with the eye roll, sis?"

Confrontation with Quinn never did any good. Shannon always ended up feeling like Lucky backed into a corner—

wanting to bare her teeth. But it was futile to fight back. "Nothing."

"Are you jealous of Marshall and me?" Quinn advanced, which left Shannon retreating, the backs of her knees hugging the twin bed behind her. "I've seen the way you look at him, you know."

Oh, that was rich.

But before Shannon could respond, Quinn plowed on, her hands working overtime as they waved. "When he got home from your place yesterday, he decided he didn't feel well enough to go to the beach. What did you say to him?"

He hadn't gone last night? She couldn't help the smile curving on her lips.

"See? I knew it. You like him."

"Quinn, just stop. I know the truth."

Color drained from Quinn's face as her hands dropped. "What did you say?" The low words emerged from between her clenched teeth. Her eyes flashed white-hot. But, for a moment— here and then gone—there was also something almost … vulnerable.

Scared.

But what did Quinn have to be scared about? She had an amazing job, lived a fashionable life in New York City, and could land any man she wanted.

Still, she was lying for a reason. Shannon just wished Quinn would confide in her about why. "Marshall told me the truth." She stepped forward.

Quinn held her ground, her chin held high, no trace of trembling.

"I know your real boyfriend broke up with you." Shannon kept her voice as steady as she could despite some shaking, as if speaking to a spooked horse. "Why are you lying to all of us?"

Her sister's chin dipped for a split second as she studied Shannon. Her mouth opened then closed before she shook herself and narrowed her gaze again. "Don't worry about it. Just keep your mouth shut, all right?"

"You should come clean. Tyler, Mom, Dad ... they won't care that you—"

"I'd hate for it to come out that you were attempting to steal my boyfriend. Imagine how that would look to the foster care agency."

"What?" Shannon blinked. "But I'm not. You don't even have a boyfriend."

"Appearances are all that matter in this world, little sister."

"But—"

"I'm glad you see this my way." And without a backward glance, Quinn stormed from the room.

With a gasp in her throat, Shannon sank back against the bed, head spinning, limbs numb and depleted. Somehow, despite her deeper desire to connect, she'd just picked a fight with the woman who never lost one.

CHAPTER 9

*H*e'd managed to successfully avoid Quinn all day, but Marshall's luck likely wouldn't hold much longer.

He opened the back seat of Shannon's Corolla and pulled out the last two desserts—some sort of cream pies. With as much care as possible, he shut the door with his foot and walked from the Walker Beach Community Park's car lot back toward the huge grassy area where Shannon and several of her cousins bustled, putting the finishing touches on tonight's picnic event.

They'd taken over the ramada, where picnic tables were lined with a variety of foods prepared by family members who had already started to arrive—fried chicken, pasta salad, baked beans, onion dip, potato salad, and chips. And that was only for the main course. The dessert table had already begun to fill with cakes, cookies, and every other sweet thing under the sun.

Even though the Bakers had taken over quite a bit of the park, a few other families currently lingered. Kids swung and played tag on the playground on the other side of the ramada. Across the park, a youth baseball team practiced on a field with floodlights that would turn on automatically at dusk, which was still several hours away.

Amazing how much open space there was here—room to breathe, to think, to gather—compared with Manhattan. Marshall couldn't deny the strange ache that deflated his chest at the thought of leaving here on Monday—in just four days. Of course, that wasn't all due to the beauty of California.

Not the beauty of the town anyway.

As he approached the ramada, his eyes sought her out. And there, her hair blowing about her cheeks as a draft caught it, Shannon was writing something on a clipboard. She glanced up.

His heart gave an extra tap.

"Are those for the pie-eating contest or dessert table?" she asked.

"Not sure. They're the last ones from the back of your car."

"Okay, the contest then." Using her pen, she pointed toward a table in the grass. "Can you put them over there, please?"

Today she was all business, laser-focused. At some point, though, maybe he'd get to spend some time with her. He'd be lying if he said he hadn't pictured them latched together during the three-legged race. Or maybe instead, he'd steal her aside and talk about yesterday—and the fact he'd almost kissed her.

The fact he still wanted to. More than anything.

But after she'd outmaneuvered him yesterday, things had gotten less personal, just like now. They'd talked through event details and then she'd kicked him out so she could go to her aunt's house and prep for this morning's bridal shower.

Could be she just had her mind full with the event details. Maybe she'd be more open to talking once her part was finished. Then he could finally figure out what she was thinking.

And hopefully ease the ache in his chest—the one that was halfway sure the part of him that was starting to open up to someone was about to be crushed.

He shot her what he prayed was a casual grin. "Absolutely I can put them over there. What do you need me to do after that?"

"We're almost done with the setup." They'd been at it for a few hours at least, once she'd come over from Bella's bridal shower. "Can you double check that all the equipment is in the right bin for each of the games?"

He saluted her. "You got it, boss."

"Thanks, Marshall." She stuck the pen in her mouth, biting down on the end for a few seconds before lowering it again. "Hey, so I have a confession to make."

The cold of the pie tins seeped into his palms. "Okay."

"Um ... Quinn knows that I know." Swiveling, Shannon took off in another direction.

Well, okay then. At least it was all out in the open—among the three of them, anyway.

As he walked the pies over to the table sitting in the shade of a huge elm, a horde of Bakers shouted their hellos to him, including Shannon and Quinn's parents.

These were good people and he hated lying to them. But now that Shannon knew, could he convince Quinn to call the whole thing off? Maybe Shannon was right and he didn't need her sister's recommendation for the promotion anyway.

Marshall settled the pies on the table next to about a dozen others. A few flies buzzed around and he shooed them away. As he glanced up, Quinn approached. "Marshall."

Just the person he'd been hoping to avoid—and yet, needed to talk with more than anyone. "Hey, Quinn."

"Nice to finally see you. Don't think I haven't noticed you disappeared on me the last few days. Oh, and by the way—you told Shannon?"

He sighed. "Come on. I need to check a few things. We can talk as I work." Turning, Marshall walked toward the game course, where several blue plastic tubs were lined up on the sidelines. "I told her the truth because I like her, Quinn. And I didn't want to lie anymore."

"Of course you like her. Everyone likes her." Quinn put her hands on her waist. "But you need to hold up your end of the deal if we are both going to get what we want."

"And, what, exactly is it that *you* hope to gain from all of this?" Marshall peeked inside the first tub. Velcro latches for the three-legged race, check. "What do you care about so much that you're willing to lie to your family? Doesn't it bother you? It bothers me, and until this week, I didn't even know them."

She looked away, huffing. "That's my business, okay?"

"You keep saying that, but your business is affecting a lot of people. Including me."

"I didn't hear you protesting when I promised to help make you a director."

He ran his hand along the nape of his neck. "Yeah, well, that was before I knew them. Before I knew *her*."

But apparently that was the wrong thing to say, because Quinn's lips twisted into a grimace. "What is it about my sister that everyone finds so appealing? Because let me tell you this— no one is that good or kind or ... whatever."

"She is."

"Fine, you want to carry on with Shannon? Be my guest. But stop doing it so publicly. Your little stunt at the talent show the other night had people talking. Then someone saw you leave Fleur de Lee with a bouquet of flowers last night. Rumor has it that you were in trouble with me and buying apology flowers." Quinn flung her hands in the air. "Guess they weren't too far off."

Right. No secrets in a small town. "I don't want to hurt you, Quinn, but I think I need to back out of this deal. I just can't do it anymore. And I'm not sure if I need it, to be honest. Yeah, I'm not the only one competing for the position, but my work ethic and commitment to the job should be the reasons I get it—not because I made a deal with someone in upper management."

When Quinn had presented him with the opportunity, Marshall hadn't stopped to consider how bad it sounded. After all, everyone made deals to get ahead in the corporate world, and he was sick of being left in the dirt.

But now, saying it out loud made him shiver with disgust.

"Oh, you need me. Especially after the win that Dylan pulled off this week."

"What are you talking about?" He'd been so wrapped up in the reunion—okay, in Shannon—that he hadn't logged into email or social media since right after he'd arrived in California.

Quinn pulled her phone from the back pocket of her jeans, thumbed around for a moment, then flipped it for Marshall to see. On the screen was an Instagram photo showing Dylan and several of their coworkers out at their favorite local pub clinking their drinks together. The caption read "Celebrating a huge win with the team."

"What win?" *Please don't let it be what I think it is.*

"I talked with Kelly"—their admin assistant—"and she said Dylan landed Bask, Inc."

Marshall stumbled backward from the tubs on the ground, his chest pinching. "How?" That was *his* contact, not Dylan's. And he'd been close to landing the account. So close.

"I guess the rep called, found out you weren't in the office, and Dylan swooped in and got them instead." Quinn's nose scrunched. "Personally, I think that was really bad form on his part. He should have forwarded the request to you."

Groaning, Marshall punched his right fist into his left palm, which burned with the contact. "I can't believe this is happening. I worked for months priming the pump. How could he do this?"

"That's business, Marshall." Stepping closer, Quinn placed a hand on his upper arm. "You do what you've gotta do to survive. And that's all you and I are doing here. Surviving."

The words sounded right, justified. He wanted so badly to believe them.

If only they didn't sound so much like something his father would say.

Maybe they were more alike than he wanted to admit.

"Excuse me." His stomach grumbled. "I think I'm going to be sick."

∼

The picnic had gone off without a hitch.

Thank goodness something in her life was going right. Shannon scrubbed a hand through her hair, which was a tangled mess thanks to the consistent breeze that had blown throughout the afternoon and into the evening.

Now, at ten, the last of the family volunteers waved goodbye, leaving only Shannon and Marshall to finish the cleanup. Her feet ached from running around all afternoon and the forced participation in every event. Since Gabrielle was tired and not feeling well, Tyler had claimed Shannon as his partner and stuck to her like glue. It had been oddly sweet, though she suspected he had ulterior motives.

She bent to pick up another piece of trash and stuffed it into the huge black garbage bag filled to the brim in her hands. Glancing around the park, she didn't see any more. Good. The sooner they finished, the faster she could get herself soaking in her bathtub at home and forget how much it had hurt seeing Marshall tied leg to leg with Quinn, his arm snaked around her waist during the race they'd dominated.

Shannon lugged the trash bag back to the ramada, where Marshall was washing down the brown plastic picnic tables they'd used for the food buffet. "Once you're done, I think we can go home. Thanks again for your help."

She tried to keep her tone professional, but to her ears it sounded stiff, almost cold. Still, keeping him at arm's length was the only way for her heart to stay intact.

"Of course." And then he flashed her a tentative smile that spread slow and steady across his face, revealing those dimples that were her Kryptonite.

Her knees shook. From exhaustion.

Or not.

But at least, after today, she'd be too busy with Ben and Bella's wedding festivities—the decorating and rehearsal dinner tomorrow, the wedding itself on Saturday—to spend much time around Marshall and Quinn. And the whole town would be at Sunday's Fourth of July festival, which meant the possibility of being in direct contact with either of them was practically nil.

She just needed to survive the next few minutes alone with him, and Shannon Baker would be home free. Then she could go back to trying to brainstorm ways to get back in the foster care agency's good graces. She'd already left a message begging for a chance at another interview, but had yet to hear anything back.

Once her head was clear and her heart full, she could focus on Noah—the most important male in her life.

"Well ... goodnight."

"Shannon." The light from the tall lamps surrounding the edges of the park reflected the golden tones in Marshall's eyes. "Do you have a minute to talk?" He looked so dejected standing there, a rag hanging limp in his hands, lips cocked into a semi-frown before she'd even uttered a reply.

She had to be honest, though. "I'm not sure that's a good idea."

Marshall set the rag on the table and stepped forward, snagging her free hand. Her other gripped the garbage bag, hanging on for dear life.

"Fine." He paused. "If you won't talk, will you run with me?"

"Run?"

He leaned forward and unclenched her fist from the bag. Then, his hand moved slowly toward her side and Marshall St. John poked her. "You're it."

"I'm sorry?" Shannon couldn't help a tiny grin.

His fingers settled just above her right hip. "As in, tag, you're it." Then he tickled her, stealing her breath as involuntary laughter came swift and strong before he took off running toward the empty playground.

For several long moments, she stared at Marshall. Then, laughing on purpose this time, she stole after him, ditching her flip-flops, the cold grass squishing between her toes as she ran.

He climbed the rungs of a ladder and hopped onto a platform then raced across a bridge. Her breath coming quickly now, Shannon switched directions. When he saw her plans, he paused then fled back the way he'd come.

Oh no, he didn't. The breeze slapped Shannon's cheeks as she plopped down on the bridge and shimmied underneath the railing, landing in the soft sand before standing again and tearing after him.

Rounding the playground, she climbed a ladder and cut him off right near the tic-tac-toe board. "Gotcha!"

He didn't stop but barreled right into Shannon, hugging her, both of them laughing as they caught their breath. His heartbeat thudded against her ear, and his shirt smelled like his cologne.

She should leave right now, before she did something she'd surely regret.

Instead, she glanced up at Marshall, and in a flirtatious tone she didn't know she possessed, teased him. "See, small towns have their charms too. Where else could you have an entire park to yourself? Definitely not in New York City."

But rather than the smile she'd expected, his features darkened. He released her and turned toward a tall orange slide that led back to the ground.

Problem was she didn't want to go back to the ground. She wanted to stay right here, up in the clouds.

"Hey." She touched his shoulder. "What's wrong?"

It took a few moments, but eventually he faced her again. "Sorry." Marshall sat on the platform, orange bars at his back, and she joined him. "You're right. Small towns have some great benefits. But there's also a darker side to them, one people don't talk about."

There was some serious hurt lingering in his eyes—hurt she longed to soothe. Reaching for his hand, she slipped hers inside. "I'm here if you want to talk about it."

Now that they sat, her whole body shivered. She settled her toes just underneath Marshall's legs, which stretched out in front of him. Then she leaned against him.

Natural as could be, he placed his arm around her shoulders and tucked her against him. "Small-town gossip ruined my family."

"How?" Sure, Carlotta Jenkins—the queen bee of the Walker Beach gossip circuit—knew everything about everyone, but to Shannon's knowledge the stuff she said was never malicious. Or maybe Shannon was just naive.

"I told you my parents divorced, but not *why.*" A sigh shuddered out from him, rumbling beneath Shannon's ear. "My dad was up for reelection, and a rumor circulated that my mom had cheated on him with multiple men. These guys all denied it, of course. My mom denied it too, but my dad started to believe it. Oh, he defended her in public, but the things he said to her at home when he thought I wasn't listening ..."

Oh, Marshall. Shannon squeezed his hand in solidarity. "That's awful."

He gazed up at the sky dotted with clouds that blocked the light from the moon and stars. "That's not even the worst part. My mom got depressed, unable to get out of bed, and Dad worked more, if that were possible. All of their friends took sides against each other. It was like a civil war in Blakestown."

His thumb skimmed the top of her hand, and more goosebumps raced up her back even though she was nestled solidly in Marshall's embrace. Still, she used the excuse to snuggle closer. "I can see now why you dislike small towns so much." Shannon placed her other hand on his chest, which echoed the rise and fall of her own. "And then you moved to New York, right? Did your parents share custody?"

"I spent summers back in Iowa for the first few years, but I was so mad at my dad that those months were pretty miserable. After that, he pretty much gave up on me and let me live full time with Mom."

"Do you and your dad still talk?"

"Not since my mom's funeral."

What? Not once had Marshall indicated his mom had died. "Marshall, I'm so sorry."

"I was twenty by that time, and there was a car accident. She died on impact, so at least she didn't suffer. But man, how she suffered in the years leading up to that. In a way, she died long before that accident. The happy mom I knew, anyway."

His voice cracked. "So when Dad showed up at her funeral in his crisp suit, all put together and pretending to grieve, I ... I just couldn't take it, you know? Something inside me snapped and I told him to get out. That he'd killed her. That if he hadn't allowed us to be chased out of town nine years before that, she never would have been on that icy road in New York in the first place. And then I said that I never wanted to see him again."

Tears streamed down Shannon's face, and she couldn't say a word—just slipped her hand around his waist and squeezed.

"It was a terrible thing to say. I know that." Marshall laced Shannon's fingers together with his own. "But he didn't even argue with me. Just left, like I was doing him a favor by telling him to go."

"And you really haven't seen him since?" She couldn't imagine.

"No. Last I heard from one of my friends back in Iowa, my dad eventually moved to Los Angeles to work as an attorney at a big law firm."

Ah. Now she understood why California was not his favorite place. "It's probably weird being in the same state as him, huh?"

He shrugged. "Yeah, I guess. I try not to think about what it would be like to waltz into his office and give him a piece of my mind."

"I can't understand why he'd move so far from you." What parent would do that?

"He's just a jerk who only cares about himself." Marshall shook his head. "When Mom and I first moved away, I begged him to come with us to New York, to forget everything that all those Blakestown gossips had said. But he wouldn't do it. Either his reputation and his job mattered too much to him … or we didn't matter enough."

"But I'm sure he loved you, in his own way." What parent didn't? But then again, Julie Robinson had left sweet Noah behind for her own selfish reasons.

"If so, he had a funny way of showing it." Marshall shifted on the platform. "I sometimes worry that I've turned out exactly like him. Even when I don't want it, his voice is in my head, telling me to go further, to do more. To *be* better. But I want to scream back that *he* wasn't better. That his reputation meant more to him than his family, the people he supposedly loved."

What could she say to ease the ache in his voice? As she considered her next words, crickets chirped, surrounding them with a natural chorus that was always there but only audible when they quieted to listen.

Shannon sat up so she could look Marshall in the eyes, so he could see her face and know she meant what she was about to say. "Marshall St. John, I may have only known you for a little while, but my heart feels like it knows yours. And what I see is a good man. Maybe your priorities are a little skewed, but the great thing about priorities is they can be changed."

She pointed gently at his chest, then spread her fingers over the place where his heart beat steadily beneath. "You have the power to change them. So did your dad. But you aren't him. You can make a different choice. Choose a life steeped in love, not achievement. Because at the end of the day, achievement will only get you so far, and you might not like the loneliness of that place once you get there."

The sharp look in his eyes speared her. She inhaled the smell of loamy dirt rising from the park. "Now come on. I'll race you to the swings." Easing past him, she took the slide, which twisted a few times before her toes hit the grainy sand. She took off running toward the three metal swings blowing in the breeze, their chains squeaking ever so slightly.

In a few moments, she sensed him behind her and picked up the pace. Just before she reached the swings, he caught her around the waist and tickled her again. Then he touched the cold tip of his nose against her neck, hugging her close from behind.

"Thanks, Shannon." His warm breath caressed her before he let go and settled himself onto a swing.

"You're welcome." She sat on the swing next to him.

They rocked in silence for a few moments before Marshall spoke again. "So you got to hear all of my family drama. How about you?"

"Despite being a large family, we Bakers are actually pretty close. Not a lot divides us. Although ..." Shannon attempted a solemn face.

"Go on."

"There is one thing that we can't agree on." The corners of her mouth twitched, but she held back the laugh itching to come out. "Half of us prefer Captain America—the best Avenger —and the other half think Thor is the greatest."

Marshall chuckled as his body swayed in the swing. "But then there's Ironman ..."

"Oh no. He's much too sarcastic for my tastes." She shook her head, grinning. "Though, confession—my cousin made me watch all the movies last year. Before that, I knew nothing about any of them."

"I'm thoroughly impressed by your knowledge, then." He tilted his head, smile disappearing. "But in all seriousness, what's up with you and Quinn?"

Oh. *That's* what he'd meant by family drama. "Um. Well. We're just so different." Understatement of the year.

"Seems like more than that." He frowned. "Is the weird vibe between you because of Cody?"

Her eyes narrowed at his mention of the guy she'd partnered with for a high school Spanish project her sophomore year—the guy she'd thought herself in love with.

The one Quinn had suddenly taken an interest in and, basically, stolen from Shannon.

Not that he was hers to steal. Probably he'd never liked her, despite the fact they'd held hands once. But then Quinn had come around, batting her eyes and showing off her midriff in her little cheerleading uniform, and Cody Briggs was on to the prettier Baker sister.

The more confident one.

The better one.

But although it stung, there was another, more powerful memory that stuck out—one she hadn't thought about in a long time. "Cody was part of the rift between us, but it really started before that."

Dangling her feet in the sand, Shannon swiped her toes backward and forward. It felt so stupid now, but it had been a big deal when it happened, and she could see now that some of her resentment toward Quinn had begun that night. "My dad took us to this daddy-daughter dance when I was in third or fourth grade. I was so proud of my pink dress—it made me feel like a princess, you know?"

At Marshall's encouraging nod, she continued. "But then Quinn came out in her dress and looked ... well, like a queen." And it wasn't just because her face had finally recovered from all the post-accident surgeries she'd had and was no longer puffy and red-hot. There was just something about the way her sister carried herself that evoked a regal air.

"What happened then?"

She cleared her throat. "At the dance, my dad danced more with Quinn than with me, but that was partially my own fault. I was a bit of a wallflower, if you can believe it."

"Not you." Marshall's teasing grin gave Shannon the courage to smile back.

"Crazy, right? Anyway, my dad promised me the final dance, but when it came time for it, my sister convinced him to dance it with her instead." A sigh slid from her lips, her twitch of a smile gone. "I shouldn't have been surprised. Quinn always got what she wanted. Still does."

She remembered how it had felt, standing on the sidelines, watching what was supposed to be her dance with Dad happening without her. Tears had streamed down her cheeks and onto her outfit, ruining the fabric of her new dress.

"He asked if I minded, and of course I said no, because I hate fighting. But deep down I think ... it just really hurt that he picked her." The bumpy loops of the swing's chain dug into her palms where she gripped them. "Ever since that moment, I've known one thing about my sister. That when push comes to shove, everyone will pick her over me. It's just the way it is."

Marshall stilled on his seat then stood. His hand reached out, snagging her chain and stopping the movement of her swing as he leaned closer. Shannon swallowed past the sudden dryness in her throat and lifted her gaze.

There was that look in his eyes again. Serious, zeroed in, crinkled around the edges. His nose only inches from hers, he finally spoke. "Not everyone."

And then his lips found hers in the sweetest, softest kiss she could have imagined. Her hands continued to grip the chains of the swing, anchors in the storm swirling inside of her, taking over.

Marshall tipped his head away for a moment, looking at her deeper, fuller before he swept back in for another kiss, this one to match his gaze. And Shannon couldn't help but let go—of the chains, of the restraint that had held her back all her life.

Standing, she looped her arms around his neck. His kiss was fire and water and breath and life and everything she needed to keep going, to believe that she was more than what she'd always believed. That this man with such a heart and zest and intelligence would want *her*—incredible.

While his hands held her firmly at the waist, Marshall's lips followed the curve of her jaw before trailing down to the warm creases of her neck. A soft moan rumbling in her chest, Shannon ran her fingers through the tuft along the edge of his hairline just above his neck, and his grip on her tightened before he pulled back.

"Shannon, what are you doing to me?"

Reality flooded back to her. Senses returned—more than the flashing heat and cold that left her feeling numb like frostbite had taken hold. Shannon blinked.

No. She wasn't ready to start thinking about the what-ifs or what tomorrow would bring.

So she tugged his head back down to her mouth and, just before giving in to another kiss, whispered a reply against his lips. "What I've been wanting to do since I first met you."

Then she plunged back into the abyss.

Oh, my.

What a lovely way to drown.

CHAPTER 10

*M*arshall didn't know how all of this was going to play out—only that he had to see Shannon again.

Pronto.

Which was why he'd shown up on her doorstep at eight o'clock this morning, a cup of Earl Grey in tow.

She'd looked so adorable—and confused—as she stood there in her fuzzy pajama pants and white tank top, hair thrown up in a messy knot, her face scrubbed clean of any makeup. If *that* was her fresh-out-of-bed look, whew ... he was a goner.

But he'd already known that last night, after he'd kissed her as thoroughly as he'd dared before she'd dropped him at Tyler and Gabrielle's house just after midnight.

Now, they stood hand in hand at the top of a bluff, watching a few surfers ride the morning waves. So far he and Shannon were the only visitors at the hulking white lighthouse about five miles north of town, but more would likely show up in an hour when tours officially began. And while the idea of learning the history behind the light station intrigued him, he'd rather spend every spare moment with the woman beside him.

Who knew how many they had left.

He pushed the thought from his mind and tugged Shannon down the miles-long path that wound throughout the surrounding seaside area. Long beach grass waved in the wind, tickling Marshall's legs as they ambled down the pavement. Huge rock faces emerged along the coastline, and big swells of water rose up and seemed to disappear as they splashed against the boulders.

"I haven't been out here in a long time. This is incredible." Shannon stopped walking for a moment as she took it all in, her gaze roaming the landscape—the utter barrenness and yet fullness of it all.

He lifted their joined hands and kissed her knuckles. "Yes, it is."

She turned, their eyes connecting for a beat before she smiled and shook her head. "I meant the view."

"So did I."

Rolling her eyes, she shoved him playfully. "You did *not* just use that cheesy line on me."

His free hand found his heart and pressed against his chest. "Cheesy line? I'll have you know I meant every word."

"They always do."

"They?" Snagging her waist, he pulled her close, setting his nose against hers. "What other men are spouting their cheesy lines at you? Do I need to mark my claim?"

And then, as if someone had pricked a pin in her, Shannon deflated, her shoulders drooping, gaze lowering to his chest. "I just watch a lot of romance movies, that's all."

"Hey." He stroked his thumb across her cheekbone and tucked a rogue strand of hair behind her ear. "I was just kidding. I know things are really new between us and didn't mean to imply we're exclusive or anything."

Even though I want to be.

Never been so sure of anything, really—although he'd stayed

up half the night trying to reason out how a relationship between them would ever work. Besides their differences, there was the little fact they lived three thousand miles apart.

Shannon bit her lip. "That's not it. It's more that you think you have any competition." Tugging out of his grip, she stepped off the path and wandered closer to the shore.

"Shannon, wait." Catching up to her, he touched her elbow. "Did I say something wrong?"

Finally, after a beat, she turned. "I've never had a boyfriend. Never dated. And last night ... that was my first kiss."

"You're kidding."

Her cheeks seemed in that moment to be sunburned. "I know it's pathetic, to be twenty-seven and never—"

"That's not what I meant." He took her hands, looped them up and over his neck, and drew her close again. "I meant I can't believe that someone who kisses as good as you do hasn't had any practice before."

And what did that mean for future kisses? Hopefully he'd get to find out.

Shannon's jaw fell open, her mouth forming an O.

"Then again, I'm happy to help you practice some more." He grinned. "If you'd like."

A shy smile replaced her look of astonishment. "I would like that. Very much."

Marshall gladly complied, kissing her as lightly as possible before deepening their connection. At her small intake of breath, his chest expanded. How was he so lucky a man, to be the only one in the world who had ever tasted the honey mint of her lips—to experience the sweetness that was Shannon Baker?

Marshall ended the kiss then pressed his lips to Shannon's hairline before hugging her again. She could probably hear the pounding hammer that was his heart, but at the moment he couldn't be bothered to care about that.

"Shannon. This ... it feels ..." The last thing he wanted to do was scare her away with the depth of his emotions, but he also didn't want to lose her out of some misguided sense that he shouldn't speak up.

"I know."

Of course she did, because more than anyone in his life, she got him. How was that even possible after so short a time?

Maybe he should stop trying to figure it out and, instead, just be grateful for it.

They started walking again, still off the beaten path as they crested a sandy ridge and stopped. Marshall inhaled a sharp breath. Spread below them were hundreds of fat brown seals with strange faces, their noses drooping down over their hidden mouths like elephants' trunks. The animals mostly lay along the surf, bathing in the sunlight, their grunts echoing out toward the sea.

"Whoa." The breeze nipped at his cheeks, but Marshall couldn't turn away. "I'm locked up in my office so much that I tend to forget how awesome nature is. But it never ceases to amaze me."

"It's easy for me to take it for granted, having lived here my entire life." This time Shannon reached out for his hand. "I get so used to the view and forget there's a whole world out there just waiting to be discovered. A world beyond all the problems facing me right now—the adoption, Quinn ... whatever this is between us."

"You see that as a problem?"

"Don't you? Everyone here thinks you're Quinn's boyfriend. How do you think they're going to react if they see us together?"

"Yeah, you're right. That *is* a problem. But I'm not sure what to do about it. I don't want to keep pretending, but telling the truth would probably cause more trouble between you and Quinn." And yeah, he wouldn't get that promotion either. But as he stared into Shannon's eyes, he realized she had been right last night. He didn't have to be like his father. If he had to choose between Shannon and the promotion, she would win. No question. "The only other option that I see is for Quinn to tell the truth herself. Unfortunately, I don't think that's going to happen."

"I know." Shannon looked away, lips pursed but not tight. More like resting, considering. "She's so desperate to keep her secret that she threatened me."

"What? How?"

"Yesterday at the shower, when I told her I knew the truth. She implied that if I told anyone, she'd make sure the town thought I had broken you guys up—which in turn would ruin my chance of adopting." She shrugged a shoulder. "If I still have one."

"That's messed up." He inhaled through his nose. "It almost makes me want to tell everyone, just to spite her."

"Don't think I didn't consider it."

"Aw, so you're not a *complete* saint." Marshall winked at her.

Shannon poked him in the ribs, a hint of a smile lingering for a moment before disappearing. "We can't expose Quinn. It would embarrass her."

"Seems like it would serve her right."

"Probably." She frowned. "I just wish I knew why she hates me so much. Why she has always seemed so set against me. We're sisters. We're supposed to be on the same team, but she's never acted like she wanted that. I know we're different, but …"

"You *are* different. She's mean and hateful, and you're the exact opposite."

"I know she acts like that, but there has to be a reason, you know?"

"Sure, there's a reason. There always is. But people can choose how they react to those reasons, and she's chosen poorly."

"Maybe I wasn't a good enough sister. Maybe I should have—"

"Stop. Don't let her behavior be a reflection on you." He tugged her close again. "Honestly, I think she's probably jealous of you."

"Why? There's nothing to be jealous of."

"False." He kissed her softly on the lips.

Her cheeks pinked in that adorably humble way she had. "Look at her, at her life, and then me and mine. Don't get me wrong, I love my life, but it's not glitzy or glamorous. It's quiet and comfortable, but that's never been Quinn. She was made for the spotlight."

"Some spotlights are brighter than others, but they burn out a lot faster. Maybe she's figuring that out."

"Maybe." She snuggled into his embrace, watching the waves, their hearts beating together in time. "So ... what now?"

"I don't know." And he hated that. "The only thing I do know is that I don't want to say goodbye after this weekend."

"Could ... you stay longer?"

"I can see about that. I have some leave saved up." He studied her, another idea swirling in his head. *Just ask her.* The howls of the seals urged him on, an encouraging ensemble. "Since you're still off work until the school year starts, how would you feel about coming to New York for a bit?"

"I don't want to say goodbye either, Marshall." She stared at the collar of his shirt, unwilling or unable to meet his gaze. "But things with Noah are so uncertain right now. I don't know that I should leave."

"Even for a few days?" And as soon as the words left his mouth, he tasted their selfishness. "Never mind. Of course you don't want to leave."

"I *want* to visit you. Maybe if the whole Noah situation wasn't happening ..." She shrugged. "But it is, until I hear otherwise."

"I understand. Really." He squeezed her, tossing on a gentle smile he didn't feel. "We'll figure it out. I promise."

How? He wasn't sure. In the short term, he could make a few trips out here. But in the long term—if there *were* a long term—how would that work? If she adopted Noah, then she'd want to stay here since his grandma was in Walker Beach.

Which meant Marshall would have to move. And it wasn't like he loved his job so much he wasn't willing to do that if this developed into something deeper. Not like he couldn't find another marketing job closer to Walker Beach.

But he couldn't quite let go of the nagging whisper in the back of his mind—the one that reminded him of how it had wrecked his parents' relationship when both of them weren't willing to give in equal measure. The one that wondered if Shannon was using Noah as an excuse because she didn't really believe this might be worth the risk.

That *Marshall* might not be worth the risk.

Ah geez, he was turning into an emotional sap. Pushing the negative thoughts away, he focused on the woman in front of him. She was real and solid with not a whisper of *what-if*.

And his world was more beautiful with her in it.

Love was on her mind today—and not just because she was busy decorating for Ben and Bella's wedding.

As family members buzzed all around the Iridescent Inn's courtyard, Shannon hummed to herself. She stood back to examine the placement of the three hurricane vases of varying sizes on the round table in front of her, then stepped forward to adjust some of the flower petals she'd scattered around them. The sun was at the tiptop of the sky, providing light but thankfully not enough heat for her to worry that the thick cream-colored candles might melt within the textured glass. Beneath the candles, which sat on coated metal cups inside the vases, she'd artfully placed a mixture of sand, seashells, and white flowers.

Bella had given her free rein with these centerpieces, so Shannon had spent hours over the last few months scouring the Internet to come up with the perfect look for the reception tables. Her mom always teased that she'd become a preschool teacher so she could do arts and crafts full-time, and maybe that wasn't far from the truth. Shannon just loved making things beautiful. And weddings were her favorite.

Maybe someday, it would be her own wedding she'd be decorating tables for. Marshall's face flashed in her mind, and she couldn't help touching her lips as the memory of his kisses just hours ago flooded in. And when he'd suggested a visit to New York, she'd wanted to drop everything, forget her responsibilities, and say yes. To not care what anyone else thought. To leave her comfort zone and see if she could fly on the wings she'd had all her life but never used.

Could she actually be falling in love? It was a ridiculous thought, right?

But stranger things had happened.

"That looks wonderful, honey."

Her humming ceased as Shannon spun to find her mom at her elbow. "Thanks, Mom. I think the decor turned out okay."

Mom slipped an arm around her shoulders. "It's perfect. The right mix of elegance and casual beach theme that Bella wanted. You have a gift, sweetie." She squeezed then looked down at her. "Something about you is … different. You seem more confident. Maybe that's it."

Yes, because for once, she hadn't been the sister in the shadows. Someone had seen her there, coaxed her out onto the figurative stage of her life.

With another squeeze, Mom moved on to help Aunt Lisa with something in the inn's kitchen. In a few hours, Shannon would have to run home for a shower, then be back here for the rehearsal and on to the Walker Beach Bar & Grill, which Ben and Bella had rented out for the rehearsal dinner.

But for now, Shannon continued with the tables, smoothing out a few wrinkles from the tablecloths and straightening silver chargers on the table. After she'd finished, she found her purse sitting on one of the chairs and fished her phone from inside to check the time.

One missed call and a voicemail.

She inhaled quickly. It was from the foster care agency.

With shaking fingers, she lifted the phone to her ear and listened to the message. *"Hi, Ms. Baker, thank you for your call a few days ago."* A woman's pleasant but tired voice echoed across the line. *"I apologize that I'm just now getting back to you, but it has been a busy week. Regarding your questions, you have no need for concern. Mr. Peters is notoriously ... well, even though he wrote up a few marks of concern on your file, you passed your interview just fine. I'm sending details about next steps to your email today. Thank you for your commitment to becoming a foster mom. Please let me know if you have any questions."*

Shannon couldn't help but squeal. Three women glanced up from the garland they were twisting around the banister of the outdoor staircase. Jenna Wakefield was one of them, and after a word to the other two, she stepped away.

"Good news?"

"I didn't bomb the interview like I thought. I'm still able to move forward so I can adopt Noah."

"Yay!" Hopping on the balls of her feet, Jenna pulled Shannon into a quick hug. "That's amazing. Congratulations."

"Thank you. It's such a relief, honestly." Although it definitely meant a busy schedule was on her horizon. There would be classes every week she'd need to attend, a room to finish decorating, and lots of other steps that would take up her time, especially after she returned to work once school started next month.

How would she ever make time for a long-distance relationship too?

"Uh oh, what's that frown for?" Jenna tapped a finger against her chin, her dark bangs falling across her eyes for a moment till she flipped them back.

It might feel nice to get someone else's opinion about the whole thing and verbally process what she was feeling. Shannon nodded toward the beach. "Walk with me?"

"Of course."

They stepped out of the courtyard, through the gate, and onto the path leading down to the inn's private beach, where tomorrow a team of volunteers would set up chairs and anchor a simple arch to the white-brown sand several feet from the spot where the water met earth. For now, though, the beach was deserted.

Turning, they headed down the beach toward the B&B on the north side of the Iridescent Inn. Over a year ago, a developer had purchased both of the surrounding inns but eventually sold them, one to a local proprietor and the other—the Barefoot B&B—back to the town.

Jenna's gaze fixed on the Barefoot, which grew closer with every step. "Did you hear someone bought this old place?" Even from here, the weather-worn paint and patched roof were visible. Though she hadn't been inside, she'd heard the same earthquake that had damaged the Iridescent Inn last year had also wreaked havoc on the Barefoot B&B.

"I wonder who."

"No one knows. It's a regular Walker Beach mystery. I'm sure Carlotta will sniff it out soon enough, though." Jenna stuck her hands in the back pockets of her jean shorts, her long muscular legs proof of the hours she spent surfing. "So ..."

"So." Shannon stopped. "Marshall kissed me."

"Whoa. Details!"

With a smile that she couldn't help, Shannon plopped down on the ground and filled Jenna in on everything that had happened.

"You've had a busy few days." Picking up some sand, Jenna let it filter through her fingers before lying on her back.

Shannon laughed. "I really have."

"So what happens now? I mean, he goes home in a few days, right? And the whole town still thinks he's dating your sister."

"Don't remind me." Shannon lay back too, and the warmth of the midday sand soaked through her clothing into her skin. "I don't know what's next. He might extend his trip. And I might go out for a visit. Eventually. But long term ..."

"Have you talked long term?" Jenna was up on her elbow, staring down at Shannon with an arched brow. "You barely know him."

"Not exactly." But they hadn't needed to say the words aloud, had they?

"Shannon. This ... it feels ..."

"I know."

Shannon stared up at the clouds that had moved in. When they were really little, she and Quinn used to make a game out of finding shapes in the sky. Naturally, Quinn had always been the master, finding the best ones—elaborate elephants, graceful-looking girls in tutus, a heart within a heart.

"The clouds tell us our future, you know." Quinn had said it in her most grown-up voice. And, no questions asked, Shannon had believed her.

Of course, now she knew it wasn't true, but back then ... she'd been sure her sister had put the clouds in the sky herself. Shannon had never been able to see what Quinn had seen anyway, but the fact Quinn insisted she saw them made them real.

126

"This is your first real relationship, isn't it?" Jenna's voice brought Shannon back to the present.

"Yeah." If she could even call it a relationship yet. "So it's crazy to think long-term at this point, right?" Covering her eyes for a brief moment, Shannon shook her head.

"Not necessarily. Supposedly some people just know." Jenna snorted. Guess she didn't subscribe to that theory, but then again, Liam's dad was a piece of work from what Shannon had heard. Abusive, in jail, and he'd left his teenage girlfriend high and dry when she got pregnant. "Just … be careful. I don't want you getting hurt because you've built it up larger in your mind than he has in his."

"I can't help but think long term." Shannon groaned. "All my favorite movies have ruined me for anything but a completely magical love story."

Her friend patted her arm. "And you'll have one. It just might not be with Marshall."

"You're right." Sighing, Shannon frowned. "When I really think about what it would take for things to work out, there are some obstacles that seem insurmountable."

"Like what?"

"Well, obviously he lives in New York. If I adopt Noah, I would never move him away from Mary, and I'm not sure Marshall would ever move here." After what he'd told her about his family's past, she could completely understand why he might be averse to the idea of living in a small town again—especially one in the same state as his father.

Most likely, she was getting ahead of herself anyway. Shannon was just a small-town girl with nothing but love to offer. Right now, Marshall seemed to want her in spite of that, but when he returned to the glamour of New York City, would he still?

"That *is* a big obstacle. But the most obvious one is that your entire family thinks he's in love with your sister."

"Yeah. Then there's that." And the complication of distance seemed like a tiny thing in comparison.

"Of course, if he just came clean …"

Shannon winced. "He kind of suggested it, but if we tell the truth, Quinn gets upset. And an angry Quinn isn't an adversary I want."

Squinting, she searched the clouds for a sign, a clue about her future—a fruitless effort. All she could make out was some sort of bird.

"And Marshall also doesn't get his promotion if you out Quinn."

"I don't think that matters to him anymore." At least, she really hoped it didn't. He hadn't said as much, but she also hadn't asked.

That didn't mean she didn't wonder, deep down.

But she'd just have to trust him, trust what they had. "The problem is, if the truth comes out, Quinn all but threatened to tell the whole town I stole him from her and make sure it gets back to the foster care agency."

"So much for sisterly affection and loyalty." Jenna sat up and pulled her knees to her chest. "I'm sorry, Shannon."

The bird in the sky sharpened, its head flattening and widening until it became very distinct—an owl. Wait, wasn't that a bad omen or something? "Love isn't supposed to be this complicated, is it?"

"You're asking the wrong woman on that one. I haven't dated since Brock." Jenna's lips flattened as she gazed out across the ocean. "But I will say this. You deserve a guy who is all in, Shannon. One who's willing to sacrifice for you, who will stand up for you. You deserve someone who will fight for you."

The owl in the sky lifted its wings, flapping once, twice in agreement.

Oh man, she was seeing things. Shannon blinked, and the figure dissolved into a blob of regular old cloud.

CHAPTER 11

*T*he wedding day was supposed to be all about the bride, but Marshall couldn't keep his eyes off the third bridesmaid.

From the moment that Shannon had walked down the sand-strewn aisle in a strappy light purple dress that swished around her sandaled feet, his gaze had been glued to her. He'd forced himself to turn his attention to Bella as she walked down the aisle arm in arm with her mother.

The bride had stayed laser-focused on her groom. Marshall had sneaked a peek at Ben, who'd wiped at the corners of his eyes a few times before Bella reached him.

And now, while the evening sun cast shadows along the beach and a redheaded woman off to the side of the arch strummed a guitar and crooned about not being able to help falling in love, Ben and Bella lit their unity candle then joined hands. Ben said something and Bella laughed softly.

Marshall's gaze tiptoed to the right once more, past Bella's maid of honor—Jessica, if he remembered right—and Ashley, and finally settled on Shannon. She clutched a bouquet of white flowers and watched the wedding with tears in her eyes. Man, she took his breath away, and it wasn't just the way the silver necklace she wore draped across her delicate collarbone, or how the tiny purple flowers woven in her hair enhanced the softness of her curls.

It was everything about her—her aura, the love she demonstrated for her family and friends, the way she could so completely take the focus off of herself and what she might be feeling and put it on others. He hadn't had a spare minute to talk with her since their trip to the lighthouse yesterday morning, but he was sure that Shannon had put every effort into giving Bella whatever she needed to make this day a success. As he'd walked through the courtyard on his way down to the beach, he'd seen the evidence right there in front of him—it all looked so professionally decorated, so beautiful.

Just like Shannon. Just like her soul.

Quinn squeezed Marshall's hand. He glanced at her and had to look away from her accusing glare before he said something he'd regret. Thankfully, he hadn't been with her much this morning. She'd been off helping before the wedding, and he'd been drinking beer and watching a baseball game with Thomas and some of the other men.

It had been ... really nice, if he were honest. To be one of the guys. To not be striving just to get people to like him or his projects. It had been easy, shooting the breeze, yelling at the foul balls, clinking their glasses together during one of the Dodgers' home runs.

If things worked out with him and Shannon, this could eventually be his family.

How would they feel about him if they knew he was lying, though? If they knew that he was really thinking of Shannon even though he was sitting here holding Quinn's hand?

Marshall couldn't take it anymore.

But what could he do? He and Shannon had both agreed not

to expose Quinn. Marshall's fingers tugged at the collar of his shirt then paused.

"The only other option that I see is for Quinn to tell the truth herself."

What if he could convince her to do just that? Maybe she'd have compassion for him and Shannon. Not that she was known for it, but she couldn't be that selfish, right? Shannon was her sister, after all. If Marshall had any siblings, he'd do anything for them.

The music faded and the Bakers' cousin Spencer, the pastor at Piedras Blancas Church, stepped under the arch once more. "Well, guys, it's that time."

Ben squeezed Bella's hands, and they grinned at each other.

"By the power vested in me by God and the state of California, I now pronounce you husband and wife. Ben, kiss your bride!"

"Yes, sir." Ben tucked Bella into his arms as if handling precious china then kissed her. And kissed her. Whoops and cheers broke out in the crowd, and Ben waved them off with one hand. Finally, Bella playfully pushed him away, adjusted her veil, and shook her head, laughing.

"It's my pleasure to introduce to you for the very first time, Ben and Bella Baker."

Recessional music flooded the outdoor speakers, and the bride and groom joined hands and strolled down the aisle, Bella holding her bouquet aloft like a trophy. The rest of the bridal party followed—Jessica on the arm of Ben's friend Evan, Ashley on her husband Derek's, and finally Shannon with her brother Tyler.

Marshall winked at her as she passed. A small smile creased her lips and she averted her eyes.

"Could you be any more obvious?" Quinn's voice hissed in his ear.

He sighed. Something had to change. Tonight.

Pastor Spencer dismissed the crowd back up to the reception area. As Quinn began to turn, Marshall caught her elbow. "Can we talk?"

She studied him for a moment before nodding. "Of course." Grabbing his hand, she tugged him toward the south part of the beach, where a bluff covered in flowers and sand extended over the water. "Just make sure you smile and don't look upset, or people will think we're fighting."

"Fine." For the first time today, he looked at Quinn—really looked at her. She had the straightest posture of anyone he'd ever known, and her sleek brown hair glistened in the waning sunlight. With her black sheath dress, smooth makeup, and super high heels—how did she walk on the beach in those things, anyway?—she was every bit as stylish here as she always had struck him in New York.

Was she really as shallow and arrogant as she seemed? Or was there more beneath the surface, some depth or vulnerability he could appeal to?

"Quinn, we need to end this charade."

For a split second, Quinn blanched. "We literally have less than forty-eight hours until we go home. You didn't strike me as a quitter, St. John."

"It's not about quitting. It's about doing what's right." Turning, he tucked his hands into the pockets of his trousers and watched the water beating the rocks. "And the truth is what's right."

"Not always. Sometimes the truth hurts."

He peeked at her out of the corner of his eye. She stood next to him, arms crossed over her chest, frowning as she took in the same sight he did—an ocean spanning the whole horizon, pulsing with life.

Maybe she saw something different than he did.

But he couldn't settle for someone else's view of the world anymore. "The lies are hurting someone you love, Quinn."

"Are you referring to my sister?"

"Yeah." He paused. "You do love her, right? Because she loves you. She refuses to call you out because she doesn't want to embarrass you."

"Well if she's fine with it, then why aren't you?" Leaning down, she plucked a long pink flower up by the roots.

"I wouldn't say she's fine with it. And I'm not either. Because ..." He trailed off. Even though she held all of their fates in her hands, it was really none of Quinn's business.

"Wait." She faced him, absently tugging off a petal from the flower and letting it drift to the ground. "I know you like Shannon, but you don't actually think you have a future together, do you?"

"We definitely don't if you won't tell the truth. Otherwise, the lies will always be between us, and people will think the worst of her."

"And you."

"I don't really care about that."

"Regardless, me telling the truth isn't what determines if you guys have a future or not." Quinn ripped another petal from the flower head, crushing it between her fingers. "My sister will never move to New York, and I know you'd never move to this dinky town with no job prospects. You're too smart for that."

Marshall wanted to grab the mutilated flower from Quinn's hand and shove it back into the earth where it belonged. "I think she'd consider moving someday if she weren't in the middle of adopting."

"Maybe if the whole Noah situation wasn't happening ..."

Well, okay, not in so many words, but it was implied. Wasn't it?

"Really." It was a statement, not a question. "She never once even *visited* New York while Tyler lived there. Me, I can understand, but she and Tyler are really close. Not even after his divorce did she come, because she's a scared little homebody who won't leave the comfort of what she knows."

"You don't know her like I do."

"No?" The flower fell from Quinn's hand, only one petal left on the stalk—left to shrivel and die, plucked and nearly naked, without purpose. She took a step and crushed it beneath her heel. Didn't even seem to notice, but somehow Marshall felt the heaviness of it in his chest. "Maybe you're right. But if her own flesh and blood wasn't enough to get Shannon out of Walker Beach, then do you think she'll do it for a man she just met?"

Air cut off from his lungs, and he coughed. How did Quinn always know exactly where to attack to gain the full advantage over her opponents?

His cheeks burning, Marshall opened his mouth to argue, but she placed her fingers over his lips. "Remember. Don't look like we are fighting, or I'm going to have to kiss you again."

His lip curled in disgust—not at the suggestion, but from the vitriol she spewed. "How in the world are you related to Shannon? What happened to you? Did New York change you into this person who doesn't care about anyone but yourself, or have you always been like this?"

Quinn blinked at him, lips tightening.

Whoops. He hadn't meant to say all of that. Then again, maybe someone needed to put Quinn Baker in her place.

"And guess what? I know that Shannon doesn't want you embarrassed, but I don't really care anymore. I'm telling people the truth." He motioned toward the wedding guests still lingering on the beach. "And I don't care how it looks."

He shoved past her and marched down the bluff.

"Marshall, wait! Please."

He pivoted, an eyebrow raised. "What?"

Quinn pressed the palms of her hands to her cheeks, her brow wrinkled as she stared at him. "You can't. I …" A sob rose from her throat and she spun, facing the ocean once more.

That was new too, but he wouldn't put it past her to be the kind of woman who manipulated with tears. His jaw stiffened as he ambled back over and stood beside her.

For several minutes, they were both silent, until finally, she spoke. "Marshall, you can't tell people the truth. I'll become the laughingstock of Walker Beach. People here already hate me. I can't stand the thought of them laughing at me too."

"They don't h—" Marshall paused. Because if these were Quinn's true colors, then maybe the people here really *did* hate her.

"Exactly." Her eyes growing red, Quinn pushed her hand against the tip of her nose.

"So you lied. You own it, apologize, and move on."

"I didn't just lie. I was dumped. Humiliated. Edward was supposed to come to the reunion to meet my family. I basically implied to my parents that I was nearly engaged. Instead, hours before, he told me he didn't love me enough to meet my family. That he'd only really seen us as a way to fill his off-work hours."

What a jerk. Then again, he'd never liked the guy. "Sounds like you're better off."

"I'm not even that upset about the relationship ending, so I guess I felt the same way about him. More mad that he humiliated me and made me stoop to such desperation that I involved you in all of this." She groaned. "I'm so messed up, Marshall."

"We're all messed up, Quinn. That's part of being human."

"Shannon's not." Quinn wiped beneath her eyes, the edges of which were rimmed in dripping mascara. "She's little Miss Perfect."

"Funny. I think she believes the same thing about you."

Tilting her chin up, Quinn swallowed hard. "Back to the matter at hand. I'd never be able to show my face around here again if people found out I brought a fake boyfriend home. It's so pathetic." Her eyes finding the horizon again, Quinn stroked the scar that began at her hairline and ran through her right cheek to her jaw. "The problem is, I don't have a life to go back to in New York."

Huh? "I don't understand."

She closed her eyes. "You're going to hate me when I tell you this. But ... I got demoted a few days before we came out here."

"You what?"

"Hugh brought me into his office and told me that he was moving my reports to another manager. Said even though I am great at my job, I'm not a people person."

"Ouch."

"Yeah. And I may have let my pride get the better of me, because I immediately put in my two weeks' notice." She grimaced.

"Wait, so ... if you're leaving the company, how do you expect to help me get a promotion?"

Quinn remained quiet a moment too long, her eyes burning a hole in the ground.

"Oh." She didn't. "You lied to me too, huh?" Unbelievable. "Why? Because you knew I'd do anything to get what I wanted?"

Like Dad.

"No!" Quinn placed her hand on his arm, fingernails clinging to the wool fabric of his suit jacket. "I knew you were really nice, and probably the only one who would do this for me. And yes, I shouldn't have lied to you, but I needed a win after basically losing my job and my boyfriend in a matter of days."

"I still don't understand why that necessitated lying to me."

"I'd already told my parents that I was bringing my boyfriend, already had implied that things were going really well between us ... and after missing Tyler's wedding, I knew I couldn't miss the family reunion too. But I also couldn't show up empty-handed."

"Your family is great. They would have understood."

"Maybe. Probably. But they expect one thing from me —excellence."

"Quinn, *my* dad truly demanded excellence of me. To the point where I don't even know if he loved me." Okay, he hadn't intended to go *that* deep. But whatever. "You're lucky to have parents and siblings who love you even when you're a jerk to them."

She stiffened, but didn't disagree. "Maybe you're right. Maybe I just expect excellence in myself. But I failed." Quinn shook her head really slowly. "They'd have seen that. And I didn't want their pity."

"Why not?"

"Because I've had enough of it to last me a lifetime."

That didn't make sense. "So that makes it okay to lie to everyone? To manipulate *me*?"

"No. It doesn't." She sighed. "I'm sorry, Marshall. You have to believe me."

Actually, he *didn't* have to. And he didn't want to.

But something was shifting inside of him, dousing the coals burning in his chest as Shannon's voice played on a loop in his head. *"I know she acts like that, but there has to be a reason, you know?"*

"Even if I believe you, that doesn't change what needs to happen now. You have to tell your family the truth."

Quinn blew out a breath before squaring her shoulders. "I will. Soon. I promise."

"When?"

"I don't know. Just let *me* be the one to do it. Please." She rubbed the corner of her eye. "I'm the one who made this mess, and I'm the one who has to clean it up."

He could respect that. At the very least, he could accept it, even if he preferred for the truth to come out sooner than later.

"On one condition—you promise not to slander Shannon or hurt her chances of adoption."

Shaking Marshall's offered hand, Quinn nodded. "Looks like we've got a deal."

He only hoped she wasn't the devil in heels.

CHAPTER 12

*H*er cheeks hurt from smiling.

And not just thanks to all the photos required of the bridal party, but also because love was in the air—and it was beautiful.

Shannon stood inside the courtyard strung with a plethora of tiny white lights overhead and watched Ben and Bella dance across the wooden dance floor they'd installed for the occasion. The tables were filled with loved ones finishing their dinner of steak and salmon, laughing, having a grand time just being together. And none of the ladies could stop oohing and aahing over the beauty of Bella's drop waist gown, with its sweetheart neckline and draped tulle body, as well as the adorably intense looks of devotion Ben kept fixed on his new wife. Shannon hadn't even known her cousin could waltz, but apparently he'd learned.

Love did that—it changed a person.

Shannon grinned again as Ben gathered his bride in his arms and dipped her. The music faded and applause erupted.

"Give it up again for our beautiful bride and her handsome husband." The DJ, a woman in her thirties with a tasteful nose piercing and short hair, spoke into her microphone from the sound booth set up near the courtyard fountain. "Now Ben and Bella would love for any couples out there to join them on the dance floor for the anniversary dance."

Some good-natured groaning ensued as women tugged their men up from their seats. While the music to "The Way You Look Tonight" flowed from the speakers, Shannon took the opportunity to snag a Sprite from the bar. The cool liquid soothed her parched throat and she leaned against the stone wall, watching all the couples she loved make their way to the dance floor.

Mom and Dad, aunts and uncles, Madison Price and Evan Walsh, Ashley and Derek, Tyler and Gabrielle—though the pregnant woman looked fairly uncomfortable despite the flats she wore, poor thing—and so many more.

A contented sigh puffed from her lips, down deep from her very soul. These were the people she loved, all gathered together in the place she loved. Maybe at the next town wedding, she'd be out there with Marshall and Noah.

Their own little family.

"You deserve a guy who is all in, Shannon." Was Marshall that guy? Only time would tell.

She continued to scan the dance floor as she sipped her drink, and her eyes landed on Quinn and Marshall. It was just for show—she knew that—but her insides twisted at the sight of Quinn's arms looped around his neck, of his fingers skimming her waist. Thankfully, they stood a respectful distance apart and looked deep in conversation.

"Shannon, there you are."

She jumped at the words, her hand flying to her chest as she turned to find Piper Lansbury standing beside her, a pad of paper and pen in hand. The thirty-something newspaper reporter wore wide-leg black trouser pants and a smart white collared shirt, her brown hair pinned back into a sleek ponytail and a large black camera around her neck. She must be covering the wedding for the local paper. "Hey, Piper. How are you?"

"I'm all right." Piper lifted an eyebrow. "How are *you*?"

Goosebumps traveled the length of Shannon's arms, and they had nothing to do with the light breeze coming up from the water in the distance. The reporter, who was best friends with Shannon's cousin Samantha, had always made Shannon a bit uncomfortable with her directness. Between that and her uncanny ability to ferret out the truth in every situation, Piper really was made for big-city reporting, but for some reason had returned to Walker Beach after college.

And right now, she was looking at Shannon with a mixture of sympathy and shrewdness. Did she somehow know the truth about Marshall and Quinn?

If so, that would not end well for anyone.

Shannon cleared her throat. "Happy for Ben and Bella, of course."

"Oh. Right." Piper waved her hand, dismissiveness in her tone. "I meant how are you doing now that Julie Robinson is back in town? I know you wanted to adopt Noah."

Shannon twisted to face Piper, the motion sending splashes of her drink onto the stone pavers at her feet. "What?"

The reporter frowned. "Julie is back and seeking custody of Noah. The social worker didn't tell you?"

"No." Shannon hadn't heard from Miranda all week, but the woman knew about her intentions toward Noah. She gripped the cold cup in her hands so hard the plastic creaked beneath her fingertips. "Are you sure?"

"Yes. I was at the memory care facility visiting my grandpa when Julie came to see Mary." Piper's nose crinkled.

Shannon's ribs and lungs squeezed, making it difficult to draw in more than a scant amount of air.

Julie was back. Back for Noah. But she'd abandoned him.

Surely they wouldn't grant her custody, right? "How did she look?"

Tapping her fingers along the edge of the camera, Piper studied Shannon. "Good, actually. Much more put together than I've ever seen her. I heard she got a job as a CNA in Los Angeles and is going back to school to be a nurse." She paused. "I'm sorry, Shannon. I thought you knew. After I saw Julie, I called Noah's social worker to get an update. As a reporter, you know."

In front of them, the song ended and couples started leaving the dance floor. Quinn and Marshall parted ways, and Marshall headed toward the drink station. His eyes found Shannon's and they narrowed. He mouthed, *You okay?*

Her whole body urged her to seek comfort in his arms, but she couldn't. Not here, where all of her family would be able to see them. She looked away, her lower lip trembling, swallowed. "What did Miranda say?"

"She spoke off the record, of course …"

"I won't spread any rumors, I promise."

Piper's jaw ticked. "Oh, I know. It just makes me mad. A mom can leave her child behind and then get a steady job, come back, and snap! All is forgiven. She can have another shot at being a mom. Gotta love the justice of our system." The sarcasm in her tone contrasted with the upbeat song that underscored it on the speakers.

Shannon's head pounded in time to the beat. "I don't understand how this can be happening." Poor Noah. If Julie was back only to jerk him around again …

How would he survive it?

Setting down her cup on the tray of a passing server, she covered a sob that escaped through her fingers.

Piper flicked her ponytail over her shoulder as she shook her head. "It's not fair. To Noah *or* you."

Someone shouted Piper's name from the other side of the crowd. She put out her hand as if to pat Shannon's arm, but stopped halfway and then dropped it. "Are you sure you're okay? I've got to go take some photos for the paper, but ..."

"I'm fine. Really." It was a lie and they both knew it, but it wasn't like Piper and Shannon were really friends. "Thank you for the information."

"If you need help digging up dirt on Julie, I'm happy to help. As far as I'm concerned, she doesn't deserve a second chance." With her pen and pad at the ready, Piper set out into the crowd.

Before she could make a scene, Shannon whirled, fleeing toward the inn, where she could shut herself away in the bathroom for a bit and cry. But at the bottom of the stairs, Mom intercepted her. "Dear, I'm gathering our immediate family up so we can get a photo together. Meet just outside the gates, by the trees near the beach in about ten or fifteen minutes, all right? It'll take me that long to find everyone. I have no idea where your father disappeared to."

So much for time to cry. Shannon wasn't one to normally care about things like smudged mascara or red blotchy eyes, but if she knew her mother, this picture would find its way onto the mantel for all to see. "Sure, Mom."

Before Mom could get a closer look and realize something had upset her, Shannon moved back through the crowd, sticking to the fringes as much as possible to avoid conversations with people she didn't have the composure to talk to right now. The news about Noah and his mom sat as heavy as bricks on her chest, threatening at any moment to squash the where-withal from her mind and body. She needed air, and waiting under the large trees that surrounded the courtyard was as good a place as any to get it.

Shannon pushed through the wrought iron gate and stepped into the soft, clean sand. The full moon and its blanket of stars made for a beautiful wedding backdrop, the heavenly decor outshining all of Shannon's votive candles and flowers and vases—or enhancing them, really.

Finding the largest of the surrounding oaks, whose leaves made a canopy overhead, Shannon leaned against the scratchy trunk. She closed her eyes and willed the tears to stay put, at least until her mom's required photograph was over. The sound of the water lapping against the shore mingled with the strains of "Unchained Melody" drifting on the summer breeze.

A soft caress touched her upper arm, and she opened her eyes to find Marshall there. The pure adoration and concern in his gaze was all it took for the tears to start. Without a word, he tucked her into him, the silk of his tie smooth and cool against her cheek.

His head bent low, near her ear, and after a few moments, he spoke. "What's wrong, love?"

Pulling back, she looked up at him, at the way his eyes drank her in, and all thoughts of others and Quinn and long-distance and Noah and everything else fled. Shannon pushed up on her toes, flung her arms around his neck, and kissed him like none of that existed—like tomorrow didn't even exist.

She couldn't taste him deeply enough—the nip of salt from his steak, the tang of his beer—and her hands couldn't feel him close enough. He responded in kind, pressing her back against the tree trunk, feathering his lips across her jaw, whispering promises and the depth of a budding love that scared her.

"Shannon." His head finally pulled back just a bit, though his arms remained firmly ensconced around her. "What's wrong, love?"

His repeated question made her want to burrow into him all the more, but she suddenly became conscious of their position —how just on the other side of this wall, her entire family danced and celebrated. And here she stood, in the arms of a man they didn't know was actually hers.

Her temples pounded again. It was all so … confusing.

She dropped her arms from Marshall's neck, allowing him to hold her but giving them both a little room to breathe. "I just heard that Noah's mom is back in town. That she's seeking custody. And that she might …" Biting her lip, Shannon sucked in a deep breath. "She might have a really good chance of getting him back."

"Ah, Shan. I'm sorry." He took her hand and kissed her palm, his eyes roaming her face as he seemed to be considering his next words. "I know that's not what you wanted. But … wouldn't it be the best thing for him to be with his mom, if she really *has* gotten things straight?"

"No!" Her whole body went cold at the thought. "I mean, yes, of course, but …" *But he's being taken away from me.* And the loss of Noah was like an aching chasm that divided her heart. "I'm sorry. This is all such a roller coaster. First, I'm adopting him. Then I do terribly with the interview. Then yesterday I find out that I didn't fail like I thought. And now … this."

His arms traveled up and down hers, bringing warmth and a chill at the same time. "That's a lot. What can I do?"

She mustered up a smile for him. "You're doing it by holding me, reminding me it's going to be okay."

"It *is* going to be okay." He pressed a kiss to her forehead, and they stood like that for a while, so still that she wondered if it were possible to fall asleep on her feet. Because suddenly, she felt very, very tired. And at the same time, her heart was full—of grief, yes, but of the whisper of love too.

With Marshall, she could conquer all the bad.

Her fingers wound their way up his back, pressing him close again. "Marshall?"

"Yes?"

"Did you … did you see about taking some extra time off? So you can stay here and help me fight this? Or survive it, at least?" He was silent for a moment or two, long enough for doubt to slip into the crevices of her splintering heart. Maybe she shouldn't have asked. "I mean, I know you have to go back to

New York eventually, and I have to stay here to figure all of this out with Noah, but …"

"Of course I'll stay." His lips brushed hers again. "But, Shan, what happens if things don't go the way you want them to?"

An owl hooted somewhere above them. "I haven't thought that far. But if Noah's mom does get custody again, then I think going back to work will help—seeing all the familiar faces, kids who need me, you know? And of course, resuming normal family functions and not being thrown into the craziness of a family reunion … that'll help. Just taking it one day at a time, you know? To heal. To grieve. All of that."

He loosened his hold on her a bit. "Maybe it would be a good time to come visit me." His teasing smile touched the corners of his lips. "New York–style pizza and moonlit walks in Central Park are good for healing."

Oh. How she wished she could. But the thought twisted her gut. Because suddenly, New York just felt so big, so foreign, and right now what Shannon needed was the comfort of home, of her small bubble of quiet and peace.

How to explain that to Marshall, though? "I would love to come to New York, but the timing … I mean."

"Sure, maybe not right away. But once you've got the stuff with Noah resolved?"

Something in his voice—the hesitation—hinted at a deeper meaning in his question. Was he …? No. She was reading into it. Or maybe not. Maybe he really *was* asking her if she'd ever consider moving to New York. Eventually.

A shudder worked its way through her. She knew she wanted to be with Marshall, yes. But what place did a girl like her have in New York? The Big Apple was a city for women like Quinn—vivacious women who weren't afraid to flaunt their confidence. Who weren't afraid of new adventures and, in fact, relished in them.

The fear that Shannon had been trying to suppress all day

reared its ugly head once more. Because the fact was, once Marshall was back in the flashy city, he'd see that Shannon's shine dulled next to those kinds of women.

Her mouth opened, closed again. "Maybe. Yeah. For a visit."

"You don't sound so sure."

"I ... I don't know. I just ... I'm confused."

"Confused about visiting?" His arms dropped from her waist, and he took a step back. "Or about us?"

"About everything. We're just really different and then there's the whole Quinn thing ..." Her words sounded weak, she knew. And she didn't mean them. Not really.

She didn't *want* to mean them, anyway.

"I thought we talked about that. Said we'd figure it out."

"And have you?" Because she certainly hadn't.

"Well, no, but it shouldn't be up to just *me*. Unless that's your point."

He didn't understand. She'd been racking her brain too. But the only inevitable outcome she could see was his realization that Shannon didn't stack up. Guys like *him* just didn't end up with girls like *her*—not in real life.

But before she could say as much, a mask slipped onto his face, making him a stranger. No longer was he *her* Marshall, the man who had bared his soul on that playground two nights before. Instead, there stood the slick advertising executive who told people what they wanted to hear, who cared more about achievement than relationship.

Distant, aloof. Pretending.

He turned to leave.

"Wait." She rounded in front of him.

"I think you're right." A flash of agony pierced through the mask, but then was gone. "We're too different. We just want different things."

No. She wanted him. He wanted her. At least, he had.

But maybe he'd thought better of it too.

"Marshall?" Tentative, Shannon lifted her hands to his cheeks, stroking them with her fingertips.

He grasped her wrists and slowly lowered her hands from his face. "Shannon, stop." The words bit into her, like a slap across the cheek.

A throat cleared nearby.

She whirled to find her entire immediate family—Mom, Dad, Tyler, Gabrielle, and Quinn—plus the wedding photographer standing about ten feet away.

Mom's eyes flitted between Shannon and Marshall as she eased closer. "What's going on, Shannon?" The disappointment in her tone shot frozen darts through Shannon's chest. Of course she'd be disappointed. It looked like her daughter was coming onto her sister's boyfriend, who clearly didn't welcome the attention.

And the worst part—maybe that was actually true.

"Shannon, stop."

Maybe, like with Cody, Shannon had somehow misinterpreted everything. She'd read waaaaay into the situation. Maybe Marshall liked her well enough, but only as a momentary plaything. He wasn't thinking about forever. Of course he wasn't.

And there she went making a fool of herself again.

Marshall moved a few steps away from Shannon's arms, which dropped with a thud back to her sides. "Ma'am ..."

But before he could say another word, Quinn shot forward, lips pursed. "Marshall." She leaned close and whispered something in his ear.

He shook his head. "You promised."

"I'll handle it." Spinning on her heel, Quinn faced the family and the photographer. "This isn't what it looks like, okay, everyone?"

Well, that was unexpected. Maybe Quinn would tell the truth after all.

"Then what is it?" Arms folded across his broad chest, Tyler cocked his head.

Quinn paused, biting her bottom lip as she looked from family member to family member. The expression she wore was not one Shannon could ever remember seeing on her sister's face before.

Open. Raw. Vulnerable.

Mom stepped forward and placed a hand on Quinn's elbow. "Honey? Are you okay? I'm worried about you."

And that was exactly the wrong thing to say, apparently, because Quinn stiffened. "I'm fine, Mom." Stepping back, she grabbed Marshall's hand. "We're leaving now."

He frowned and glanced at Shannon, studying her—almost as if waiting for her to say something. To make a move. Part of her longed to beg him to stay, to communicate with her eyes all the things she couldn't speak.

But Cody's face flashed in her mind again, and Shannon's gaze dropped to the sand at her feet.

Marshall's sigh was audible. "Fine. But—"

"I know. I will." Quinn's reply floated by on the same breeze that stirred the bottom of Shannon's dress. "We'll see you guys later."

Then, without even looking, Shannon knew Marshall had left with Quinn. The air vibrated the emptiness in Shannon's chest. And when she finally got the courage to lift her gaze, she watched his retreating back until tears blurred her vision—and he was gone.

CHAPTER 13

*S*he had nothing left.

Clutching the baseball-shaped pillow, Shannon curled up on the full bed in her guest room—the room she'd hoped would one day belong to a little blondie who loved the Dodgers.

After forcing herself back into the wedding scene earlier tonight, she'd done her best to enjoy the rest of Ben and Bella's evening, but all she could picture was the disappointment on her parents' faces.

And Marshall, leaving.

Finally, when the cake had been cut, she'd slipped away and come straight here, not even bothering to change out of her bridesmaid's dress. The gauzy lavender material of the gown's full skirt pooled around her feet, which were tucked up in a fetal position. Lucky licked her bare toes from his spot at the end of the bed.

The doorbell rang and Lucky's ears perked up. Who would be visiting at—Shannon checked the clock on the beat-up old dresser—ten thirty-five pm? Rolling over, she faced the wall, effectively shutting out the world and the half-finished room with half-painted blue walls and half-planted dreams.

She'd had such grand plans for this room. For her life.

But now? Those plans were toast if Noah's mom got custody of him again. And based on the questioning text Shannon had sent Noah's social worker and Miranda's response, it sounded as if that were quite possible.

Supposedly, Julie had never formally given up custody of Noah, just asked her mother to watch him for an extended period of time. Then, she hadn't heard about Mary going into the memory care facility because the phone number her mother had in her own phone was old. That had also made it difficult for Miranda to find her and let her know Noah was in foster care. According to the social worker, Julie had been in AA for a year and had been planning to come back to get Noah once she had worked her program and was fully established in her new career.

There went the doorbell again. This time, Lucky bounded from the bed and ran into the hallway, his paws thundering down the stairs toward the front door. He gave a bark and then was silent. Someone—obviously with a key—spoke to him in low tones. Couldn't her family just leave her alone? Shannon rarely wallowed, but wasn't she allowed the privacy to do it if she wanted to? Needed to?

She squeezed the pillow tighter, letting the tears come.

The light flicked on overhead and someone sat down behind her on the bed. "Hey, cuz."

Ashley.

Without saying anything else, her cousin spread out beside Shannon and held her while Shannon's tears soaked the pillow. Ashley stroked her hair and hummed low and slightly off pitch.

Okay, maybe it *did* feel better to wallow when someone was there to comfort her.

Shannon turned back over and Ashley sat up, taking Shannon's hand and squeezing it. "You okay?"

"No."

Her cousin's eyes crinkled with concern. She too was still in her dress, the light purple contrasting well with her tan skin, the straps dainty against her well-defined shoulders. "Tyler said you needed me."

"Did he tell you what happened?" Her voice creaked like rusty gate hinges.

"Yeah."

"It's not what you think. I wouldn't do that to my sister."

Another squeeze to her hand. "I know. Quinn told Tyler what was really going on."

"She did?" Shannon sat up and braced her back against the wall.

Ashley settled next to her. "Why didn't *you* tell me about Marshall?" She rubbed her dangling sparkly earrings. "I thought we told each other everything."

Shannon's body tensed, but she forced it to relax. It would do no good to tell Ashley how hypocritical her comment was after she'd eloped without a word until after the fact. "Sorry."

Frowning, Ashley's eyes scanned the room—from the blue comforter still in the bag to the bucket of paint sitting on newspaper in the corner, the dresser Shannon had started to refinish, and the chair rail strips sitting flush against the far wall.

"Noah is one lucky kid, you know that, Shan?" Ashley bumped her shoulder against Shannon's. "I know you said the interview didn't go well, but—"

"Stop."

Her cousin looked at her, eyes dazed. "What's wrong?"

"Noah's mom is back. She's going to get custody again." Hot flashes pulsed against the back of Shannon's eyes.

"What? No way."

"Way." She couldn't help the bitter tone that oozed out.

"Okay, *what* is going on with you? Is it Quinn? She's the only person I know who brings the sarcasm out in you."

The fan, the blades of which resembled baseball bats, whirred above them, *flick flick flicking* air in a constant, rapid motion as if building toward something. Every now and then, it got off balance, but it always found its smooth rhythm again.

That was Shannon, except Noah and Marshall and Quinn and everything else had thrown her so far off that there was no getting back.

"No, it's not just Quinn." Pulse racing, she leaped from the bed, unable to sit still any longer. "You want to know what's going on? I thought my life was finally going to mean something, Ashley. But now, I just …" Her chest heaved as she spun in a circle, gripping her hair. Was this what it felt like to have a mental breakdown?

"Hey, hey, hey." Her cousin raced to her, snagged her shoulders, faced her forward. "Your life does mean something. What are you talking about?"

"What is life without someone or something special? Everyone else … well, Tyler has Gabrielle and they have an amazing foundation that helps children everywhere and a baby on the way. You have Derek and your own company. Mom and Dad have each other and a thriving business they love. Quinn has a flashy career and the respect of everyone in this town. Even after the truth about Marshall gets out, she'll somehow *still* have that respect, mark my words. What do I have, Ashley? Tell me that. What do *I* have?"

Shannon paused, pressing the heels of her hands against her eyes. Her breath sputtered in and out like a train attempting to go uphill. "I just wanted one thing … one thing that was going to be *my* special thing. I wanted to be Noah's mom. And then, when I thought that might not happen, at least I had Marshall, someone who I thought saw me. The real me. Not the one I try to be, just the one I really am. But like everyone else, he chose Quinn. And don't get me started on her."

"I wouldn't dare." Ashley tried to crack a grin, but Shannon wasn't in a joking mood.

"And you ... I thought we were like sisters, you know? But when you eloped, you didn't invite me. Didn't even tell me. So everything I thought about who I was or what I had, it was all a lie."

She suddenly felt light-headed. Had she really just said all of that? Yep. Every whiny, pathetic word ...

Squeezing her eyes shut, she shook her head.

"I'm so sorry, cuz." Ashley's gentle touch forced Shannon's eyes back open. Her cousin stood there, her features twisted. "I ... I didn't think about how my actions with Derek would affect you. I was only thinking of myself."

"I tried so hard to just be happy for you. And I am. Really." Shannon shrugged. "I just wish I had been there. I love you and I always dreamed of being by your side when you married your husband."

Hugging Shannon, Ashley blew out a breath. "I got so caught up in the romance of it, but I should have thought ..."

"No, I'm sorry." Shannon squeezed her cousin and released her. Making her way back to the bed, she scooted Lucky over—sometime in the last several minutes, he'd taken over half the bed—and plopped down once more. Then she patted the spot beside her for Ashley, who joined her. "It's just something I need to get over. The world doesn't revolve around me, and I need to stop taking things so personally."

"I'm glad you told me. Did it feel good to get that off your chest?"

Huh. "Yeah, actually. It did."

"Good." Her cousin's long blonde hair fell forward as Ashley played with a tassel on the quilt. "I know you hate to rock the boat, but you should speak your mind more often."

Shannon folded her legs under her and ran her hand down

the sheer material on the skirt of her dress. "I hate conflict. There's already so much of it in the world."

"I know. But sometimes conflict is a necessary part of healing, don't you think? If you'd never told me how you felt about me eloping, I wouldn't have known. But it still might have festered and grown into this huge thing that put a wedge between us. Isn't it better that I know how you feel so we can work through it together?"

"I guess. But I should have just been able to push it down, change how I feel. See the positive, you know? That's always worked before."

"Maybe it didn't work as well as you thought." Ashley paused. "But you know that what you have to say is just as important as everyone else, right?"

Shannon's fingernail snagged against the gauzy purple.

"Shan."

She sighed. "I mean ... yeah?"

"Well, I'm convinced." Ashley stuck out her tongue, and Shannon cracked a tiny smile at her cousin's teasing. "For real, though. There's so much about what you said a few minutes ago that makes me really sad. Because I don't think you see yourself the way everyone else does."

Frowning, Shannon shifted, the weight of all the labels she'd heard or knew to be true heavy in her lap.

"Shannon, you are amazing. Everyone in this town knows it. You make things beautiful. You care about others before yourself. You give and give and give and never expect anything in return. You have a gorgeous soul."

Oh, sheesh. Here came even more tears. "I don't see any of that."

"Girl! You need to stop believing those lies. Embrace the truth. You, Shannon Baker, shine brighter than anyone I know. You always have, and you don't need to be a mom or a girlfriend or anything but who you are to have an amazing impact on this town and all the people who love you ... simply because you're you."

The warm words thumped against Shannon's ribcage. But also the harsh truth. Had she been using the impending adoption as a way to find meaning? If so, she was a rotten excuse for a human being. But she did love Noah—of that she was certain.

And as for Marshall ...

"I just feel like such a mess." She sniffled, wishing for a tissue but too exhausted to get one.

"You think everyone else has it together? We don't. And if you spend your life comparing what you think you see in other people to what you know you see in your own, then you will always be miserable. Looks can be deceiving." Ashley's hands waved as she talked, true to her passionate self. "I know you've always compared yourself to Quinn, but guess what? She's just really good at putting on an act. Why else would she have lied about having a boyfriend?"

"I've wondered that too. But she'll never tell me, even if I wish she would."

"If you really want to know, maybe it's time to be vulnerable first."

"What?" Hadn't Shannon done enough by asking Quinn at the bridal shower? Pleading with her, really?

Ashley nodded. "In the name of healing, tell her how her actions make you feel—how they've always made you feel. It'll rock the boat, sure. Might even crack it down the middle. But maybe that's what it'll take to rebuild things between you. And who knows? Maybe you'll finally realize that you and Quinn aren't that different after all."

Could her cousin be onto something? Shannon's hands trembled at the thought of confiding anything in Quinn.

Whirl, clack, whirl, clack, clack, clack. The fan slowed and sped, slowed and sped.

Then—at last—smoothed out.

CHAPTER 14

*M*arshall couldn't wait to leave Walker Beach in the rearview mirror.

He kicked at the water, his toes skimming the surface of the placid ocean as it lapped against the marina dock. Well past midnight, he probably wasn't supposed to be out here, but the closed gate was hardly a deterrent and only meant to keep vehicles from entering the marina after hours.

After the catastrophe in the middle of Ben and Bella's wedding, he'd headed straight to the parking lot with Quinn. She'd promised to address the rumors that would surely begin circulating—that photographer who'd been present during the intended family photo had looked like a predatory dog with a bone clamped in its teeth.

Then, he'd left, walking the three miles back to Tyler and Gabrielle's house and stuffing his bag full of his dirty clothing, laptop, everything.

If it hadn't been so late and he had a car and they weren't hours from an airport, he'd have been on the next plane. Instead, he'd changed from his suit coat and tie, wandered downtown, and somehow found himself here, breathing in the brackish tang that personified the ocean. Halyards clanked gently against boat masts somewhere behind where he sat at the edge of the dock.

A long, singular pier. A cubicle. An apartment with absentee roommates. Didn't matter where he was. Despite lowering his defenses, allowing someone into his heart again, alone seemed to be Marshall's lot in life.

Because much as Shannon had seemed sure about seeing if this thing between them could work, tonight the truth had been revealed.

"I would love to come to New York, but the timing ... I mean."

"Sure, maybe not right away. But once you've got the stuff with Noah resolved?"

If she couldn't even commit to visiting him, no way would she ever be willing to move. She'd rather stay in this backwater town, among people she really loved, than even *consider* moving to be with him.

He'd been an idiot to think that love was worth the risk this time.

The yawning hole in his heart told him otherwise.

Behind him, the dock creaked. Marshall glanced back, saw a hulking figure approach in the dark, only the moon to light his path. What did *he* want? Probably here to smash Marshall's face in.

Not like Marshall could blame the guy. He'd warned him to be careful with his sisters' hearts, after all.

Tyler lowered himself beside Marshall. "Hey, man."

"Hey."

Shannon's brother cracked his knuckles. "So ... do you love my sister?"

Guess they were just diving in then. Kind of made Marshall respect Tyler even more. "Yes. I mean, I could see myself ..." He picked up a pebble embedded between the wooden slats of the dock and tossed it into the water. It plopped, barely producing a ripple. "But not the sister you think."

"I know."

Marshall looked at him, sharp. "You do?"

Tyler nodded. "Quinn told me and Gabrielle what was going on tonight after the wedding."

"Oh." Good. She hadn't lied about her intentions to tell the truth after all.

It had been the hardest thing Marshall had ever done, leaving Shannon behind. But he'd promised Quinn that she could handle it in her own way. And besides, he couldn't last one more minute near the woman who had shot him in the heart with her backtracking. Her "confusion."

He really needed to stop striving for something he was never going to achieve, like love, a family of his own, one that might stick by his side this time around. Better to focus on things he could control—like doing the best possible job he could, working his way up the corporate ladder.

Sure, it could be a cutthroat world, but better a cut throat than a severed heart.

If only he'd listened to himself sooner.

Tyler knocked his fist against the dock. "I was actually really happy to hear that I don't have to pummel you. Because I kind of like you, St. John."

That elicited a slight smirk from Marshall. "Good to know." Then he frowned.

"So what are you going to do about all of this?"

"Me? Nothing."

"Nothing? That's not what I expected from you." Tyler cocked his head. "You afraid what people around here will think?"

"No." Especially if he knew Shannon felt the same way he did—which she obviously didn't. He shrugged. "I just don't think it's going to work out. She wants to stay here, and I've got a job in New York. Possible promotion coming. There's nothing here for me."

"Nothing but love."

He scoffed. *Right.* "Love might not be enough."

"Then maybe it's not really love."

Marshall eyed Tyler. "Agreed." He pushed himself upright. "Thanks for the pep talk, man, but I've decided to focus on my career right now. It's just not a good time to get involved with someone who lives three thousand miles away." Turning, he walked down the dock.

Footsteps pounded the pier and Tyler was beside him again. "I was where you are once." Tucking his hands in the pockets of his khaki shorts, Tyler turned and walked backward next to Marshall as they headed toward the Berry Street house. "And I know what it's like to be afraid."

"Afraid?" Marshall shook his head, but his heart picked up speed. The sputter of the water from a nearby sprinkler filled the silence of the dark night. "I'm not afraid."

"Well, I was. And even though I'm not really a 'talk about your feelings' guy, I'm man enough to admit it."

Now he had Marshall curious. "Afraid of what?"

"I almost lost out on a life with Gabs because I worried that I wasn't enough for her. That I needed to somehow buy her love. Which was idiotic. Because all she wanted from me, was … me."

A sharp pain needled Marshall's ribs and spread across his chest. He coughed.

But no, he and Tyler weren't the same. After all, Tyler and Gabrielle had dated in high school. They'd had a history. Marshall and Shannon, well … their relationship was super new. An unknown. And unknowns left a person open to rejection. To betrayal. To all sorts of unpleasant feelings Marshall would rather not experience. It was better to end things now, before he had a chance to feel even worse than he already did.

He stopped underneath a tall lamppost, looked hard at Tyler.

"And what if Gabrielle had decided a few months in that she didn't want you after all? Wouldn't you have wanted to know then? Save yourself the grief and heartache?"

Tyler ran his fingers along his stubbled jaw. "I'm not gonna lie and say it never crossed my mind. There's always the risk of getting hurt. Still is. But there's also a lot of joy in finding love. In being loved."

That was true. The feelings he'd had when Shannon was in his arms were life changing. But even more than that, her acceptance of his past, her listening ear, the calming effect she had on him, the beauty she'd already brought to his life in one short week—those had given him more joy than any promotion or sense of satisfaction he'd experienced at work.

And yet ... "I just don't know how to get past the what-ifs."

"The what-ifs will kill any peace of mind you have, man." They started walking again, Tyler in the street and Marshall on the sidewalk. "It's like Gabrielle being pregnant. There are times I wake up in the middle of the night sweating, terrified that something has happened to her or the baby. And then there's the thought ... like, what if I'm not going to be the dad she needs?"

"I'm sure I'd feel the same way." Especially given the crummy example of a father he'd had.

"Right? But here's the thing. Just because I'm worried about what might happen or all the ways I might fail, does that mean that it would have been better for Gabs to have not gotten pregnant at all?"

"Of course not."

"Well. There you go. It's that simple. Either love is enough, or it's not." Tyler lifted his eyebrows. "Either Shannon is worth it, or she's not."

"That's not fair. It's not about *her* being worth it."

Tyler grunted. "All I can tell you is that I'm totally not worthy of Gabrielle. Not one bit. But somehow, I've been given this amazing gift. She loves me, dude, though I can't really tell you why. And I'm just living my life trying to be the best man I can be for her and our daughter. That's all I can do. That's all any of us can do."

Marshall blew out a tight breath. "I'm glad she loves you."

"My sister loves you too. Or at least cares for you more than any man she's ever known. I can see it in her eyes."

What could Marshall say? Her actions simply didn't reflect that. She'd had the chance to stop him before he left with Quinn —he'd practically begged her to with his eyes—and she'd looked away.

"Fine, man. Be stubborn about it. Don't believe me." Tyler pointed at Marshall's chest. "At this point, it's your choice whether you push her away or not. That's on you. And if you walk away, then you really *don't* deserve her."

Ouch.

The men arrived at the Berry Street house where the outside lights warmly welcomed them home. Tyler strode through the gate and whisked inside, probably headed straight for the arms of his beautiful wife—the one he wouldn't have if he'd stayed on the same course, stubborn and unwilling to bend toward the unknown.

To lean into the potential for hurt.

Marshall held onto the pointy posts of the picket fence, staring up into the night sky. He shut his eyes against the truth, but it still prodded at him.

Because Tyler was right. It *was* Marshall's choice. He could blame his dad all he wanted for his trust issues, but really, at this point that was on Marshall's shoulders too—the decision to forgive or to let his dad's actions steer Marshall's own.

As far as he could see, there was only one way to proceed.

And he didn't like it one bit.

CHAPTER 15

*S*he'd rather be anywhere than here.

And yet, her parents' house was exactly where Shannon had committed to being on the last morning of the Baker family reunion.

A cup from Java's Village Bean in hand, Shannon ambled down the stone walkway that cut from the street through her parents' front yard. Her flip-flops smacked the soles of her feet, which still ached from all the standing and helping she'd done at the wedding yesterday.

She took another sip of her English breakfast tea, desperate for an infusion of caffeine. Ashley had stayed far too late last night, and they'd fallen asleep watching a movie. When Shannon had woken up this morning on the couch, she'd found a note from her cousin saying she'd see her at the brunch. Derek was a good guy to let his brand-new wife sleep away from him so soon.

Shannon breathed in the crisp morning air, grateful that the thought of Ashley being a married woman no longer stirred the same anger it had before. Hurt still lingered on the edges, but the talk last night really had helped.

Maybe so would the one she needed to have with Quinn.

If only Shannon were brave enough.

She pushed inside her parents' home, hit instantly with the scent of cinnamon and coffee. The rest of the family wasn't due to arrive for another hour, but Mom had requested help from Gabrielle, Quinn, and Shannon to prep the pancakes, eggs, and other food.

The wide brown tiles in the entryway gleamed, a sign Mom had been up early cleaning despite the late night. As Shannon hung her purse on one of the large hooks behind the door, her mother came around the corner. Makeup perfect, hair fresh, slacks and blouse pressed, she looked as if she'd had ten hours of sleep—unlike Shannon, who had barely glanced at herself in the mirror before changing out of her pajamas and heading over.

"Hi, honey." Mom hugged her, jasmine perfume enveloping Shannon. She pulled back, peered into Shannon's eyes. "How are you?"

"Okay." Shannon's voice wobbled with dread. How would the family treat her today? Surely the rumors about her and Marshall had spread. It was Walker Beach, after all.

"Quinn told us everything." Mom tucked a strand of Shannon's hair behind her ear. "I'm sorry for doubting you last night."

Her lids already puffy from crying so much, Shannon prayed more tears wouldn't come, though she felt their telltale prickling behind her eyes. "It's okay, Mom. I know how it looked."

"I'm sorry you got hurt too."

Ugh, she couldn't talk about this now, not if she wanted to maintain any sort of composure. "Thanks." Tucking Mom's arm in hers, she steered them both toward the kitchen. "Something smells delicious. Guess we need to finish up before the masses arrive."

"Those are the coffee cakes. I whipped them up this morning. But yes, if you could start on the pancakes, I'll have your sister fry the bacon. She and Gabrielle arrived five minutes before you."

"You got it." They rounded the corner and emerged into her parents' gourmet kitchen, complete with white marble countertops, state-of-the-art white cabinets, and stainless steel appliances.

Her curly hair up in a messy bun, Quinn stood at the huge island, cutting open packages of bacon. She glanced up at Shannon and fumbled the kitchen shears.

Gabrielle sat sideways on one of the stylish oak island stools, head in her hands.

"Good morning." Shannon set down her tea and touched Gabrielle on the arm. "Are you okay?"

Her sister-in-law looked up, cheeks pale. "Oh yeah. Just a killer migraine." She yawned. "Couldn't fall asleep after we got home last night. Baby Girl kept me up, dancing past midnight."

"You should go rest." Shannon looked over at Quinn, who avoided eye contact as she pulled strips of bacon from a package and set them on a griddle. "We've got this."

Mom lit a few cranberry candles, blew out the match, and tossed it into the garbage can at the end of the island. "Yes, dear, go into the guest room and lie down."

"I want to do my part."

"Your part is making sure my granddaughter is growing healthy and strong. Which means you need to rest." Mom walked around the island and patted Gabrielle's arm. "Now come on. I won't take no for an answer. In fact, maybe I should tell Tyler to take you home."

"That's not necessary." Gabrielle stood, wincing and clutching her stomach for a moment before breathing out. Her hands looked more swollen than usual. "He's out helping Thomas get the yard ready. I'll go lie down. But just for a little while."

"Good. Shannon, Quinn, I'm leaving you in charge here. There are a few things I need to do outside." Mom led their sister-in-law down the hallway.

Shannon and Quinn were alone.

Straightening her shoulders, Shannon headed for the large walk-in pantry and grabbed ingredients to make Mom's famous cinnamon buttermilk pancakes. She flicked on a burner, snagged several sticks of butter from the fridge, and placed them into a pot to melt.

Behind her, the bacon sizzled and popped as it heated up. Its aroma filled the kitchen.

Quinn didn't say a word.

If something were going to be said, apparently Shannon was going to have to do it. Ashley's words from last night drifted back. *"In the name of healing, tell her how her actions make you feel —how they've always made you feel."*

Whew.

Standing on the opposite end of the island from Quinn, her heart picking up speed, Shannon measured out flour, sugar, baking powder, baking soda, and salt. She took the whisk in hand and mixed the ingredients together in a large bowl. How did one start a conversation like the one she needed to have with her sister?

Maybe this wasn't the place for it. The right time.

Or maybe there wasn't going to be one. Maybe it was way *past* time.

She cleared her throat as she snagged a separate bowl. "Thanks for telling everyone the truth about ... things." To the bowl Shannon added vanilla, buttermilk, and a sprinkling of cinnamon. The spice tickled her nose.

She peeked at Quinn, who was staring at her, meat fork held slightly aloft. When their eyes met, her sister pivoted to give the bacon her full attention.

Okay, then. Shannon faced the stovetop and took the now-melted butter off, setting it aside to let it cool a bit. She turned back to her wet ingredients and took an egg in hand.

"I'm ... sorry."

Shannon's body tensed at the unexpected words. "About what, exactly?" She tried her best to keep any bitterness from her tone. Tried ... and probably failed.

"That Marshall left. I could see how you felt about him."

"What do you mean, he left?" True, Shannon hadn't seen him yet this morning, but she'd assumed he had come over with Quinn, Tyler, and Gabrielle and was helping the guys out back.

"He wasn't at the house this morning, and neither was his stuff." Quinn poked at the bacon. "And he left me a note that said he couldn't pretend anymore." She shrugged, her face emotionless. "So I assume he went back to New York."

Lungs tight, Shannon cracked the egg against the counter. The yellow yolk oozed out between the shattered shell pieces. Her shaking hands tore a paper towel off the rack and swiped away the mess.

If only life were as easy to clean up.

Ashley's encouragement nudged her again. Shannon couldn't do anything about Marshall. But right here, right now, she could maybe do something about this broken relationship with Quinn.

Boat, prepare to be rocked.

"I ... didn't know." She cracked another egg, this time successfully landing it in the bowl.

"Oh."

"Quinn." *Breathe, just breathe.* Another egg, in. "Why did you feel the need to go through the whole charade in the first place?"

Ugh, she hadn't meant to spit the words out with such an accusatory edge. Shannon grabbed the pot and poured the ribbons of yellow butter into her mix, then whisked it all together while trying to force her heart rate to slow. Once it did, she attempted a softer tone. "Because everyone around here loves you. We don't care that you were dumped. So why lie about it?"

Her sister stabbed a piece of finished bacon and tossed it onto a plate covered with a paper towel. "No, Shannon. They *love* you. They fear me. There's a difference."

Shannon's brows knit together as she combined the contents of one bowl with the other. A lumpy batter formed beneath her fingers. "I don't think that's true."

"Oh, it's true." Another piece of bacon flew onto the plate. "But I guess it's my own fault. I decided a long time ago that I'd rather have respect than pity, and that means I can't ever show weakness. Not in my job, and definitely not in my personal life."

Shannon set down the whisk and stared at her sister, whose lips were hardened into a straight line. "The truth isn't weakness. Neither is vulnerability."

"Maybe not for you." Her sister whirled mid-bacon-turn, and grease splattered across the counter and floor. "But it definitely is when you're the girl going in for the fifth plastic surgery so you don't scare other children. When you're that girl, you find a way to make others respect you—even if they never like you. And sometimes that means making up your own truth. Making people see what you want them to see."

She said it so matter-of-factly, as if talking about someone else.

But she wasn't. She was talking about herself. How had Shannon never connected Quinn's car accident and subsequent surgeries with her determination to be the strongest and the best? But Shannon had been young herself and didn't remember it being as bad as it must have been.

Clearly, it wasn't just her sister's face that was scarred from the incident. "Oh, Quinn. I'm sorry. I didn't realize."

Her sister huffed and forked up all the breakfast meat in one fell swoop. All the slices plopped onto the paper towel in a heap.

"Stop being so ... nice!" she growled. "Just for once in your life, fight back!"

"I don't want to fight." Shannon pushed the bowl aside and crossed her arms, hugging herself. "Don't you understand? All I've wanted is to connect with you. But you won't let me."

"How can we possibly connect? We have nothing in common." Despite the way Quinn's chin jutted out, her lower lip trembled. Maybe they were finally getting somewhere. "You're sweet and kind and everything I'm not. Which is fine, because I don't want to be those things. I can't."

"You could if you tried."

Quinn rolled her eyes. "We aren't all as saintlike as you. Remember Cody Briggs? You liked him and he liked you too." She pressed a closed fist against the counter, her jaw clenched. "And I set out to steal him from you, even though I didn't give a flying flip about him."

Quinn flung the truth across the room like an arrow, and it hit its target as intended. Shannon's chest ached. "I don't understand." The words gurgled in her throat even as fat tears rolled down Shannon's cheeks. "I could have been an ally, a friend. I know you were hurting, but why did you have to push me away, to hurt me on purpose?"

"Why? Because I could." She shook her head. "I'm not some puppy you can save, Shannon. There isn't a lot of hope left for me. And I'm okay with that. I've made my bed and now I'm going to lie in it. Just let me lie in peace."

Turning back to the skillet, Quinn laid out new strips of meat, mask back in place and calm as could be.

Instead of the sympathy Shannon knew she should feel, she couldn't help wanting to shake her sister's shoulders. What was wrong with her? Did she truly not think change was possible? But no, she'd clearly given up.

She didn't want Shannon's pity? Fine. Maybe she'd respond better to the truth—brutal or not.

"You know what? Forget it." Shannon threw up her hands. "I can't make you want to be sisters, to want to be on the same team as me, to want to try to be a good person. But I'm not going to let your bitterness ruin my heart. Even if you don't care about the blood, the history that we share, I do. I love you and that will never change, but I won't let your negativity run me down anymore."

And, despite the fact the pancakes sat unfinished or the way Quinn's jaw had gone slack at Shannon's declarations, she spun on her heel and waltzed out of her parents' house and into the fresh breeze of a new perspective.

Because all this time, she'd thought Quinn's life was something to be envied. The truth was, no one was perfect, and their lives weren't either. And there was beauty in that, if people could learn from their mistakes and become better for it.

What do I have, Ashley? Tell me that. What do I have?

True, Shannon might always struggle with this question, but if she could clear all the other junk away—all the comparison, all the looking at other people, all the worry over what they thought—then her vision cleared, and she saw very plainly what she had.

People she loved, who loved her back.

A town she'd do anything for.

And a voice.

Yes, Shannon Baker had a voice, and just like Quinn, she could use it for good or for evil. And that was another thing—she had a choice, about how she'd live, about the thoughts she'd allow in. From now on, she'd do whatever necessary to dim the negative voices that told her she wasn't worth as much as others, that she didn't have anything to offer, that she needed to be in the spotlight to have value.

Instead, she'd listen to the one voice that mattered. The one that told her she was a beautiful creation.

That she was … enough.

~

Maybe she shouldn't have come. Probably would have left multiple times if Jenna hadn't held fast to her arm, reminding Shannon she'd done nothing wrong.

But that didn't stop the whispers, the stares, the questioning looks the people of Walker Beach kept shooting her as she, Jenna, and Jenna's son, Liam, meandered through the Fireworks Festival crowd. Apparently, word had gotten out about Shannon "going after" her sister's boyfriend. It must have been the wedding photographer who'd spread the gossip, because Shannon's family knew the truth.

Patriotic music boomed over the loudspeakers strategically placed along the street. The event committee had closed off the middle section of the Main Street thoroughfare so food and game booths could be set up along the road. Almost every storefront boasted an American flag in its window, and someone had spent countless hours stringing red, white, and blue twinkle lights high above Main Street. They grew brighter as the evening dimmed.

The scents of cotton candy and fresh popcorn wafted from various food stands lining the street. Yet despite her many fond memories of sharing both with her family over the years, the familiar smells churned Shannon's stomach. The confrontation with Quinn this morning had her whole body on emotional overload—especially given her revelation afterward that had smacked strangely of hope.

A wave of nausea rolled through her as they passed a hot dog vendor. Yep. She definitely should have stayed home, where she could have processed her emotions in the appropriate way—with chocolate and a movie.

"Mom, I see Jared." Liam pointed toward a booth with two moving mechanical basketball hoops. "Can I go?"

"Sure, bud." Jenna dug in her purse and pulled out a neon

171

green wallet. "Aunt G and Uncle Tyler are saving us a spot on the beach to watch fireworks. Be there in fifteen minutes or I'm hunting you down."

He flicked his long brown bangs out of his eyes and snagged the money she offered. "Okay. Thanks." Racing off, he joined his friend in line.

"I can't get a rise outta that kid." Chuckling, Jenna stopped in front of the Oil Me This booth—owned by Shannon's Aunt Louise—and lifted an eyebrow at Shannon. "How are you?"

Shannon raised a vial of oregano oil to her nose and inhaled the rich aroma. "Fine."

"Uh huh."

She should have known Jenna was going to call it like she saw it. Recapping the sample oil, Shannon shoved it back onto the rack. "I *am* fine. I'm not going to crumble."

"Of course you're not. You're strong. But that doesn't mean you have to pretend to be *fine*."

"I know." Shannon sighed. "I'll be honest. I don't know where things stand with Quinn—if they'll ever be better—and I'm still heartsick over Noah. And then there's Marshall ..."

"He really left?"

"Apparently." Tyler had said as much when Shannon had returned to the brunch a few hours after leaving Quinn standing alone in the kitchen.

"Did you try texting or calling him?" Jenna moved toward the Frosted Cake's booth, where Miss Josephine and her retired husband, Arnie, were selling apple pie slices impaled with American flag toothpicks.

"He was the one who left."

"His loss then. But I'm sorry. I know how much you cared about him."

"I did." *I still do.*

But maybe some fairytales weren't meant to last forever.

Maybe they just helped people become who they were meant to be—even if hearts got bruised in the process.

"Let's grab a treat before we head to the beach." Jenna joined the Frosted Cake's line, which was about five people deep.

"Miss Shannon! Miss Shannon!"

She turned just as a small body rammed into her. Wrapping her arms around Noah, Shannon leaned down to bury her nose in his soft hair. "I've missed you, buddy. How are you doing?"

He pulled back and gestured over his shoulder. "Great! My mom is back."

About ten feet away, Noah's social worker Miranda stood with a petite woman wearing jeans and a red blouse, her long blonde curls pulled into a ponytail. She kneaded her hands in front of her and stared at Shannon.

So this must be Julie Robinson.

Jenna squeezed Shannon's elbow, a show of support.

A lump formed in Shannon's throat. "That's wonderful, Noah. Would you introduce me?"

"Sure!" Noah led her over. "Mom, this is my teacher. The one with the dog."

Julie held out her hand, which trembled slightly. "Shannon, right? I'm Julie."

"Nice to meet you." Shannon studied the woman. She'd expected sunken cheeks, glazed eyes, not this healthy-looking woman who exuded humility.

Noah left Shannon's side and snuggled up to his mom, pulling Julie's hands around him so she hugged him from behind.

Shannon's own hands tingled with the need to hold him. Instead, she folded them together and forced a smile she didn't necessarily feel—but wanted to. Because right now, it was clear that he didn't belong to Shannon. He belonged here, with his mom, so long as she could handle the responsibility. Thankfully, Miranda wouldn't let him go back to a bad situation. The

173

careful eye she currently had on Julie and the research she'd already done into her story gave Shannon peace of mind.

Julie chewed her bottom lip. "I can't thank you enough for taking such good care of my boy when I couldn't."

"It was truly my pleasure. Noah is a special kid."

They chatted for a few minutes about Julie's plans to return to Los Angeles and move her mother to a care facility nearby. "Of course, I need to prove myself to Miranda here first. Noah will continue to live with Florence for a few more weeks until she has to move, and then we will see what happens."

"I'm happy to help in any way I can." And Shannon meant it.

Then Jenna came over, a small white pastry bag in her hands, and Shannon hugged Noah and Julie both, wishing them well.

As they headed toward the beach, Jenna fished a cookie out and handed Shannon the bag. "That looked rough."

"It was." Shannon was done stuffing her emotions down. "But I truly want what's best for Noah. And if that's his mom, then I'm happy for them." Even if every step away from him physically ached.

"Do you think you'll continue with the foster process?"

It was something she'd considered, albeit only briefly. After all, Noah wasn't the only kid in need of a good home. "I'd maybe be open to it. But I think I need to take some time to process and grieve first, you know?"

"Absolutely."

Continuing down the street, they fought through spots where festival attendees stood shoulder to shoulder. It was heartening to see, considering how the earthquake nearly a year ago had harmed the town's economy. Finally, they arrived at the beach and, despite the burgeoning crowds, located their families.

Gabrielle lay with her head in Tyler's lap, and he stroked her blonde hair as they talked. Mom and Dad chatted with Aunt Lisa and Uncle Frank, and several other Bakers had claimed blankets nearby. Shannon and Jenna plopped onto the sand next to their siblings.

Shannon peeked into the bag she held, spying about a dozen cookies. "You guys want dessert?"

"Oh my goodness, yes." Gabrielle wiggled her fingers from her spot on the ground. "Baby Girl has been begging me for one of Miss Josephine's cookies all day."

"And of course my niece should have whatever she desires." Shannon handed over a double chocolate cookie.

Liam and his friend joined them with a wave. They sat next to Tyler and instantly started talking football.

The sun slipped behind the horizon completely, which meant the fireworks would begin soon. Shannon broke off a piece of a chocolate chip cookie and nibbled the edge as she sank into the moment.

There was a lot in life she couldn't control, and one of those things was other people's behavior. But here, now, peace washed over her, and it wasn't merely due to the rumble of the waves just beyond, though that always helped.

No, this time it was because she'd not let fear hold her back. She'd spoken her truths—and they hadn't shattered her world.

Marshall was her one regret. Hopefully that wound would heal in time.

Overhead, the first firework of the night exploded in the air, the heat so close it seemed to singe her skin. The crowd applauded and whistled.

"Mind if I sit here?"

Shannon glanced up to find Quinn towering over her. A purple firework backlit her as she squatted to Shannon's level.

Quinn pushed a lock of hair behind her ear and nibbled her lip, waiting for Shannon's reply.

"No, I don't mind."

"Okay." Her sister settled in beside her, knees pulled up to her chest.

They watched the fireworks in silence for the next five minutes, the top of the pastry bag gripped in Shannon's fist. But little by little, Shannon loosened her hold, and finally held it out to her sister without taking her eyes off the exploding night sky. "Hungry?"

"Um ... sure." Quinn took the bag from her fingers. "Thanks."

"You're welcome."

After a minute or two of shared watching as the fireworks displayed their glory, her sister scooted closer until their shoulders touched. "Shannon?"

She looked at Quinn. Despite the darkness, she could sense her sister's uncertainty. "Yeah?"

"I ... I do want to be sisters, if you still want that." Quinn played with the cookie in her lap. "And I want to try to be a good person. I don't really know what I'm doing in that regard, but maybe ... if you help me ..."

Shannon's heart shot off like a rocket, brilliant streaks of light flooding her veins. She hooked her arm through Quinn's. "Of course I'll help you."

"Because we're on the same team?"

"That. And because I love you."

Quinn frowned, nodded. "I'll try to be worthy of it."

"You don't have to try. Just be you," Shannon said as she laid her head on her big sister's shoulder.

"That hasn't worked out well for me so far."

Shannon laughed, and then Quinn did too. Overhead, the fireworks finale began, explosions rocking the night even as tranquility settled once again into Shannon's soul.

CHAPTER 16

*H*e'd avoided this moment long enough.

All day yesterday during the four-hour drive in his rental car from Walker Beach to Los Angeles, Marshall had fought the urge to turn around, to run straight to Shannon and beg her forgiveness for walking away with Quinn at the wedding.

For being an idiot.

For leaving her.

And then, as he'd settled into his hotel and later stood on the Santa Monica Pier last night watching fireworks, he'd had to talk himself out of heading straight for LAX. Back to New York.

But he'd made up his mind. In order to move forward, he couldn't go back. Not until he talked with his father.

"Either love is enough, or it's not."

Tyler's words had continued to haunt him for the last thirty-six hours. They were eerily similar to something Shannon had said the first day he'd met her. *"And really, all you need is love to make a thing work, right?"*

Today had dawned gray, with heavy clouds hanging in the distance. Marshall swallowed hard as he stared up at the skyscraper looming over him now, thirty or more stories high with a white facade that glittered despite the lack of sunlight.

He was about to find out if Tyler and Shannon had been right—if love could be enough. If it could overwrite the last twenty-plus years of pain.

If it could lead to some sort of healing, even if it was only one-sided.

Pushing through the hulking doors, he stepped inside the building situated in the heart of downtown. People dressed to the nines in business suits chatted as they moved swiftly to and from a bank of sleek silver elevators. Women's heels declared their owners' arrivals and beat a determined pattern against the travertine beneath them. High-powered executives with leather bags rushed past assistants balancing multiple coffee carriers.

One man knocked into a woman, causing her to drop her phone and curse at him. The man shook his head and said something to a companion, who laughed. The ding of the elevators opening and closing only added to the cacophony.

The steady stream of people, like ants racing up and down a hill, the rush, the fervor, the ambition—it all had a palpable heartbeat, one Marshall understood. One he'd allowed to dictate his own actions for so long.

But now, something about it had lost its luster. Because what had all of it gained him? If he'd gotten on that airplane and returned to New York today as planned, he'd be retreating to a life filled with … what? False hope?

The trouble was, he didn't know if staying here would produce anything better.

But he had to see. Even if the aftermath might demolish him.

As he approached the elevators, his eyes skimmed a sign that announced the location of several companies and law firms. When the elevator opened in front of him, he got in with a flood of others and jammed the button for level sixteen.

The man next to him wore far too much cologne, and in the

small space, the stuff burned Marshall's nose and churned his gut. Or maybe his roiling stomach had more to do with the fact he was about to see his father for the first time in eleven years.

The elevator shot upward and stopped at several floors before opening to the sixteenth. Marshall exited along with one other man and it took him a moment to gain his bearings. He went right and came to an office labeled Jacobson, St. John, and Associates.

After a deep inhale, he opened the door and stepped inside. The lobby—which was empty of everything but twenty chairs, some potted plants, and light jazz music streaming from hidden speakers—looked like it could belong to any other swanky firm. A large cherrywood secretarial blocked the entry to a bank of offices beyond, and the perky blonde receptionist sitting behind it beamed a grin at Marshall and asked how she could help him.

He approached. "I'm here to see Justin St. John, please." It was early, but if he knew his dad, he'd arrived at least an hour ago.

"Do you have an appointment?" Mist from a small diffuser on the receptionist's desk imbued the air with lavender.

"Uh, no. I was hoping—"

"I'm sorry, sir, but he's a very busy man." And the blonde did indeed look sorry. She leaned forward, giving him an eyeful of chest thanks to the dip in her blouse, which was on the teetering edge of professional. "But if I could get your number, I can let him know you called. Or I could just get your number. For myself." A perfectly plucked eyebrow lifted as she smirked.

One week ago, he'd have flirted right back. That's how a guy got what he wanted in this kind of setting, after all. But even that would feel disloyal to Shannon. And although she might never speak to him again, he wouldn't betray her memory like that.

Instead, Marshall frowned. "When is his next available appointment?"

The receptionist studied him for a moment, lips now pursed. She straightened and glanced briefly at her computer. "Not for two weeks."

Well, that wouldn't do. "I'll just sit and wait for him to be finished with work today."

"Sir, you can't harass our attorneys after hours. I'm afraid I'll have to call security if you don't leave."

He didn't have time for this. "Look"—he glanced at the nameplate on her desk—"Kimmy." Marshall softened his tone. "Can you please just tell him I'm here? If he can't take five minutes to see me, I'll happily be on my way."

At the mention of her name, the blonde's eyes became less narrowed, a bit more thoughtful. "Who are you?"

"His son." Marshall spun on his foot and marched to the last row of seats in the lobby, flopping into one and grabbing a golfing magazine off of a side table. He snuck a glance at Kimmy, whose eyes were round as she lifted the phone from its cradle and spoke into it.

One moment later, she set the phone down. "Mr. St. John will see you now."

"Great." Dropping the magazine, Marshall jumped up and headed toward her.

"You're really his son?"

"Yes."

She nodded, a V forming between her eyebrows. "He told me about you once."

"That's surprising." He'd always figured one reason his father had moved across the country was to forget his past, to reinvent himself. But maybe he told his coworkers the story of his ungrateful son to get pity points with the ladies.

You're not here to berate him. Remember that.

Marshall's hand formed a fist at his side. "Anyway, I appreciate you asking him to see me."

" I ... I didn't tell him who was here. Just that he had a visitor." Kimmy fiddled with an earring. "His office is the last one on the left."

"Thank you, Kimmy." Before she could change her mind, Marshall traversed the long hallway, passing a few others emerging from their offices as well as a break room where several staff members stood around a coffee pot talking.

Finally, he reached the office labeled Justin St. John, Partner. Marshall shook out his hands, ran his tongue along the top of his teeth, and knocked.

"Come in."

He hadn't heard the voice in years, and he suddenly felt ten years old again, his insides quaking at the idea that he would disappoint the man who had meant everything to him.

But no. He wasn't that kid anymore, and Marshall could choose his reaction. Fear had no place in his life. Not anymore.

Shoulders held erect, as if going into battle, Marshall opened the door. A man sat behind the desk, sipping a cup of Joe and reading something on his computer screen. He had a head full of white hair and drooping jowls. His drawn face was one Marshall barely recognized, with its wrinkles and double chin.

Gone was the well-dressed man who believed even clothing should be worn with military precision. In his place was one who wore a wrinkled button-up that looked like something he'd grabbed off the rack at Goodwill and a jacket that appeared to be at least a decade old. Stacks of paper surrounded him and the smell of stale pizza invaded the small space. It was the exact opposite of the controlled, sterile office he used to keep.

Marshall cleared his throat. "Hi, Dad."

His father looked up and flinched, jostling his coffee mug. Dark liquid spilled onto his pants and, cursing, he stood to reveal a beer gut that rivaled the Pillsbury Dough Boy.

What had happened to his father?

"Marshall?" Despite the stain soaking into his khaki pants, Dad just stared at him, blinking. "What are you doing here?"

"I'm here to say a few things." Moving forward, Marshall picked up a couple napkins sticking out from under a stack of papers. He shoved them into Dad's hands.

Dad mumbled his thanks and pressed the napkins against the stain. Then he plopped back into his chair, eyes wide. "Okay."

"Can I sit?" But before Dad could answer, Marshall lowered himself into the plush chair across from his father. His heartbeat pulsed in his stomach. "I don't want to take up too much of your time. I ..."

All the words fled his mind. No. He hadn't driven all this way to get tongue-tied. *Think, Marshall, think.*

"You look good, son." Dad's voice wavered, almost as if ...

Marshall frowned at the sight of his father with tears in his eyes. What in the world? "As I was saying ..."

"Marshall, I'm so sorry."

Huh? "Dad—"

"No, let me say this. I should have ..." His dad pinched the bridge of his nose. "I should have told you this a long time ago. And I swore if I ever saw you again, if I ever got the chance, I would."

"You had plenty of chances. You knew where we lived."

"You're right. You're right." Dad picked up a framed photo from the other side of his computer screen. Marshall recognized it as the last family picture they'd taken. And ... they looked happy.

They *had been* happy, as far as Marshall knew. His chest tightened at the way his father ran a finger down Mom's cheek on the family picture.

Replacing the photo on the desk, Dad scratched behind his ear. "My son is more of a man than me."

Had his father—*his* father—just complimented him?

Before Marshall could process any of this, Dad went on. "I take full responsibility for everything, Marshall. For believing the rumors about your mother. For caring so much about what other people thought that I let you go. For not being the father you needed."

Marshall's throat went dry.

"At first, I stayed away from you because I was embarrassed —at the scandal, yes, but also at my own actions. But that was idiotic. And I've accepted the ostracism between us as a just punishment."

Is that why he was all the way out here in California, away from everything and everyone he'd ever loved? Why he looked so far from the trim, disciplined man he'd always been?

And is this what Marshall's own future held if he went right back to the path he'd been on before Walker Beach—before a woman like Shannon had looked at him and seen more than he'd seen himself?

He shuddered at the thought.

Then he refocused on his father, who tugged at the short white whiskers on his cheeks. "I shouldn't have blamed you for Mom's death. I'm sorry for that."

"You were right."

"No, I wasn't." He gulped back a lump. "I wish you hadn't stayed away. That you'd fought for us. At least for me, even if you and Mom couldn't work things out. I'll admit, it hurt. A lot."

His dad shook his head. "I'm so sorry, son. More than you could ever know."

"I didn't come here to beg an apology from you."

"Go ahead then. Punch me." His dad held his hands wide. "I deserve much more, I know."

"I didn't come for that either."

"Then why are you here?"

Why *was* he here?

"You aren't him. You can make a different choice." Shannon's voice echoed in his brain.

He pushed out a breath from his tight lungs. "I guess ... so I don't make the same mistakes you did. The same ones I've been making."

Instead of pressing for details, his father sat back in his chair, fingers steepled together, head cocked. Almost as if he were ... listening.

But his dad didn't listen. He told. He commanded. He chided.

And yet, today, he didn't speak.

Marshall forced his knee to stop bobbing. "Specifically, I walked away from a woman who I could love, and I realized that it's because I have never resolved this thing between us. I became the one thing I never wanted to be."

His dad flinched. "Me."

"Yeah." Marshall coughed. "Look, I really didn't come to bust your chops, but—"

"No, no. You have every right. If I could do things differently, I'd tell those Blakestown gossips to ... well, you get the idea. And then, if the environment had remained toxic, I'd have taken you and your mother and moved somewhere nice and tropical, far away from all the scandal and the people who told me I'd never amount to anything." Dad paused. "That's why I stayed after you left."

"In Blakestown?"

His dad nodded. "As you know, I grew up there. What you don't know is my family lived in the trailer park. Let's just say people never thought I'd amount to anything. And then, with lots of hard work, I did. And that success—well, it became a god to me." A tear ran down his weathered cheek and Dad didn't bother to swipe it away.

The sight of that tear froze Marshall to his seat. When had he ever seen his dad cry? Not at Mom's funeral. Not ... ever.

"Son, don't let anything become more important to you than love. If you've found it, then run toward it. God knows I wish I had."

Marshall cleared his throat, eyes wandering to the ticking clock on the wall. "I don't know if I have it anymore."

"Then go and fight for it. Don't sit around wishing." His dad gestured around the room. "Otherwise, this is what your life will look like in twenty years. This is what comes of a life lived without love. A life lived with regret as the main ingredient."

Marshall sighed. "Dad ..."

He held up a hand. "Before you try to make me feel better, please know I'm not saying any of this to gain your pity. I know I don't deserve a second chance. But you, Marshall ... if you are like me in any way, I pray that it's only the good parts—the me I was before I let greed and ambition take hold. The me I was when your mother was my sun and my moon, before I let other things draw my attention away. It's not too late for you."

Whoa.

If Marshall hadn't already been sitting, he'd have dropped into his chair. The last ten minutes had cracked open everything he'd thought he'd known. He hadn't expected this reaction from his father—not at all. No, he'd pictured coming here, saying his piece to a man even more hardened by the years, and leaving with the hope that forgiveness could be a one-way street toward healing.

But now ... maybe there was still a chance for more. More than he'd dared hope.

"You're right, Dad. It's not too late." Standing, Marshall rounded the desk and, hand flexing, placed his palm on his dad's shoulder. "You say you don't deserve a second chance, but none of us do."

Marshall included.

"But that's where love comes in, right?" He took another breath of air. Of sweet, sweet freedom. "I forgive you, Dad. And I'm willing to move forward if you are."

Could things still blow up in his face? Could his father still betray him again? Hurt him?

Yes. Maybe even worse than he had before.

But Marshall couldn't control the actions of others. All he could do was be the best man possible, like Tyler had said.

He just needed to figure out exactly what that meant, go and do it, and hope for the best.

And it started with letting love in.

CHAPTER 17

The Thursday afternoon sun sparkled off the ocean and warmed Shannon's skin as she meandered down the boardwalk next to Quinn. "I can't believe you're really back for good."

A breeze whipped Quinn's curls across her face and she tugged them back with an elastic band from her wrist. "Probably not for good. I'm just ..." Her large white sunglasses covered her eyes, but Shannon could almost picture the emotions displayed there—the ones Quinn wasn't used to showing. The ones she still tried to hide.

"I know." Shannon looped their arms together. "You're still finding your way. And I'm so glad you're living with me while you do it."

"Only because Tyler and Gabrielle make me gag with their PDA." But the way Quinn's mouth quirked up in the corner told the truth—she was glad too.

It had been nearly three weeks since the Fireworks Festival, and Shannon was learning to read her sister better these days. Still, she'd been shocked when Quinn had told her she'd quit her job in New York. Instead of begging for it back, she'd finished up her two weeks online and hired a moving company to pack up her apartment and ship her stuff to Walker Beach, where she could regroup.

"I'm hoping it'll give me a chance to make amends with the rest of the family. To start fresh and figure out what I want and where to go from here."

That made two of them. Because Shannon had been on such a clear path toward adoption and now, with Noah and his mom officially reunited, she didn't know what to do except try to enjoy the rest of her summer. There were only three and a half weeks left until school started, and part of her itched to return.

She did love her job and she missed the kids. And if nothing else, it might distract her from the ache in her heart—the one that keenly noted Marshall's absence.

It hadn't faded as she'd hoped. In fact, it had only grown, sometimes a soreness and sometimes a sharp pain that would leap up and surprise her.

As they made their way to the Frosted Cake to grab lunch, Shannon felt Quinn's gaze burning into her. She glanced at her sister. "What?"

"You're thinking about him again, aren't you?"

"No." Shannon quickened her pace. "Ugh, yes. I don't want to be. Clearly, he isn't thinking about me." Wouldn't he have at least texted or called once since he'd left? But she hadn't heard a thing.

"You don't know that." At Shannon's raised eyebrows, Quinn held up her hands. "All right, it looks bad. But I've known Marshall a long time. You should have seen him before he met you. He was all business, all the time, and nothing was getting in his way. But ... I don't know, when he was with you, he was more relaxed. Focused still, but it was softer somehow. Less intense." She hip bumped Shannon as they walked. "You seem to have that effect on a lot of us."

Shannon's chest swelled with the emotions squeezing her heart. "Thanks for trying to make me feel better."

The Frosted Cake came into view, and the sisters made their way up the path leading to the door. When they stepped inside, the lunchtime crowd was in full swing. Miss Josephine's hair hung limp around her face, but the heat of the day didn't dim her smile as she helped the next customer in line.

A gaggle of women talking in a circle instantly grew quiet as the sisters entered. Carlotta Jenkins, with her huge red hair and a tight purple T-shirt, placed her hands on her hips and quirked an eyebrow in their direction. Oh goody. The head of the Walker Beach rumor mill.

Shannon looked away, pretending to study the menu even though she already knew what she was getting.

Next to her, Quinn grunted. "Are you positive you don't want me to set the record straight?"

"Yes." Sure, in the weeks since the "scandal" over Marshall had erupted, Shannon had been tempted to wipe the smug looks off of people's faces multiple times, but she didn't want people thinking badly of Quinn, especially when she was trying to make a fresh start. So she'd bit her tongue and told Quinn that if she really wanted to do something for her, that Quinn could let the gossip die off on its own. Soon enough, there would be some other gossip to take up the time and energy of Carlotta and company.

Though judging by the looks on the women's faces, the next scandal hadn't arrived quite yet.

"All right. Tell me if you change your mind." Quinn squeezed her arm. "Oh hey, here's something to distract you from the awful looks those women are giving you. I got the strangest invitation this morning. Found it on your doorstep."

"An invitation?"

"Yeah. It was anonymous and invited me to this—"

"Quinn Baker." Carlotta stood three feet away, hands on her hips. "I'm surprised at you."

Several of Carlotta's minions flanked her. "If *my* sister had moved in on *my* man, I would not be squeezing her arm—and I certainly wouldn't be living with her."

Shannon felt all the blood rush to her cheeks. A quick look at the glare on Quinn's face made her place a hand on her sister's arm. "Thanks for your concern, Carlotta, but—"

The bell jangled over the entrance. Great. More townspeople here to witness Shannon's humiliation.

But no. She didn't care what others thought about her, right? Especially when she hadn't done anything wrong. The people who knew her loved her, and setting the gossips straight wasn't worth ruining Quinn's reputation.

Her sister apparently had other thoughts. "You don't have a man, as I recall, Carlotta."

Carlotta sputtered at Quinn's response. "Well, I never ..."

"Quinn." Shannon looked at her sister, shook her head, but couldn't help a smile.

"All right, fine." Glaring at Carlotta once more, Quinn tugged Shannon out of line and raised her voice. "Let's eat somewhere else. It stinks in here—no offense, Miss Josephine!"

"Come here, sugars," the sweet owner called. They turned and found her waving a to-go bag, her own version of a glare fixed on the ring of gossips. "I saw you coming and got this going for you."

Bless her. As Quinn stepped forward to grab the bag from Miss Josephine, Carlotta's voice lifted above the crowd. "Never would have figured little Shannon Baker for a home-wrecker, would you, ladies?"

It took everything in Shannon not to run.

"Hard to be a home-wrecker when I was never with Quinn in the first place."

What? *His* was the last voice in the world she'd expected to hear. Shannon whirled to find Marshall standing toe to toe with Carlotta.

The gossip tossed him a wide-eyed stare. "Just what are you talking about?"

By now, practically everyone in the front part of the restaurant was quiet, their attention fixed on the commotion.

"I only pretended to be Quinn's boyfriend."

Shannon gave a slight shake of her head. "Marshall. Don't." She couldn't say more than that because *what was he doing here?*

And why, after knowing him so short a time, after he'd left without a word, did her entire being long to run to him, throw herself in his arms, and beg him to stay?

"Yes, Marshall. Do." Her sister waltzed toward Carlotta. "Everything he's saying is the truth. He was just a coworker doing me a favor. But when he met my sister, he couldn't help himself. Of course he fell in love with her."

Quinn winked at Shannon, whose cheeks burned. Her sister shouldn't be saying things like that. Shannon didn't know what Marshall was doing here, but his actions weeks ago had made one thing very clear—he definitely wasn't in love with her.

He wouldn't have left with Quinn if he were. Wouldn't have left without a trace, a word. Something.

Then again, she'd let her own fears get the better of her. Perhaps he had too.

Or maybe she was overthinking all of it.

But the way he was looking at her, his gaze intense, searing her to the floor so she couldn't move …

And he was here. What did it all mean?

"Quinn, while I appreciate the backup, I'd like the floor if you don't mind."

Smiling, Quinn stepped aside and gestured toward the open spot between Marshall and Shannon. "It's all yours."

"Thank you." Marshall strode toward Shannon. "The truth is, I came here a month ago with one goal in mind—to help Quinn, yes, but to help myself too." He spoke loudly, to the crowd, but his eyes remained fixed on her.

She swallowed hard.

Marshall continued. "But I had a problem. Because despite the fact I had committed to helping Quinn, I found myself drawn to Shannon. And without even trying, she's the one who stole my heart."

He stepped closer, and the surrounding smells of cake and roast beef faded as the scent of his cologne enveloped her. Marshall lifted a hand and caressed her cheek with the back of his fingers. "I know I screwed up by leaving—I know that—but do you think …" His voice lowered, the next words meant only for her. "Do you think you could ever forgive me?"

Was this real? "I …" She shut her eyes, then opened them. Yep. He was still there. "You're back. Why are you back? And why did you leave?"

Marshall brought his face even nearer. "I'm so sorry for that. I was afraid."

"Of what?"

"That you'd break my heart." He coughed. "That I wasn't enough for you."

"Marshall." She placed the palm of her hand against his unshaven jaw, and oh, how she'd missed touching him. "You are more than enough. I'm sorry that I didn't show you that."

"It was my own insecurity. Over what happened in the past, you know?"

Shannon nodded. She did know.

His hand slid around her waist. People oohed all around her. Oh yeah. They had an audience.

But at the moment, she just didn't care. Shannon looped her arms around his neck.

Marshall knew her well, though, because he took one look around and pulled her through the crowd and out the door. They hurried down the boardwalk for several minutes.

"Where are you taking me?" The words came out breathy as she laughed.

"You'll see."

People dotted the sand with beach umbrellas unfurled and beach balls flying. Some lazed about on towels, while others ran through the waves. But the only person she cared about right now was Marshall St. John—the man who had stood up for her in front of the town, claiming the truth and not caring one iota about how it would feed the rumor mill of this small town.

And when he led her to the cove where they'd first met, she remembered how she'd felt that day—scared about the future. Worried she wouldn't measure up as Noah's mom.

But then he had appeared, and she'd been Cinderella at the ball.

Was midnight approaching again? Or would her handsome prince find a way to make the time last forever?

Marshall led Shannon to the edge of the water and slipped his arm around her shoulders, staring out across the horizon as the din of the crowded beach faded and the whistle of the waves took over.

"So ..." She glanced up at him. "What now?"

The sudden flash of his dimples pummeled her. "According to my dad, we should run toward love. And that's what I intend to do. That's why I'm here, Shannon. Because more than any other person, I see the potential for that. With you."

Love ... Like Marshall, she wasn't quite ready to declare it out loud, but something deep inside agreed with the sentiment. Knew she'd do anything to be near this man. Even face her own fears of rejection.

But wait. "Your dad?"

"Yes. That's where I've been the last three weeks. I went to Los Angeles to see him."

"That must have been hard. How did it go?"

"Better than I could have ever expected." Marshall cocked his head and tightened his hold on her. "He apologized for every-thing, Shannon. It was unreal. And we spent the last several weeks getting to know each other better. Again."

"And when did you decide to come back here?"

"Three weeks ago."

She scrunched her nose. "But ..."

He laughed, grabbing her hand and turning her to face him. "I had to make sure I could be the man you needed. Someone steady and sure." The water skimmed their toes. "Someone who had dealt with the demons in my past so I didn't run away again."

Oh this man. "I'm glad you came back. And I happen to have a good chunk of time before work starts up again. Can I ... can I come to visit you in New York?" Her free hand lifted almost of its own accord, and her thumb traced his jaw, his lower lip.

He smiled against it. "I would love that. But I'll only be in New York a few more weeks."

Her hand stilled. "What?"

"I'm moving to Los Angeles."

He was? "To be closer to your dad?"

"And you."

"But what about your job?"

"Who needs a job? Someone once told me all you really need is love." His warm breath fanned her cheek as he leaned closer.

She laughed. "That person was either really naive or really brilliant."

"And also really beautiful. And someone I'd like very much to kiss right now if it's okay."

She looked deep into those dark brown eyes that had captured her from their first glance and gave a shy nod. That was all it took for him to swoop down and finally take her lips captive. She groaned at the sweetness, the slow, long melding of their mouths, the way he tasted like home.

Pulling away, he set his forehead against hers. "I missed that."

"Me too." She lifted up to peck him again. "Marshall, I don't want you to give up your job for me. I know it's important to you."

"Shannon Baker, I'm not giving anything up. By moving across the country, I'm only gaining in the ways that matter." He shrugged. "And actually, I worked it out with my boss. I'll be transferring to our LA office. It's not headquarters, and there aren't any director positions, but that's okay. I can't stand to be too far from you."

"I'm glad." She snuggled against his chest, where she fit just perfectly. "And if we decide this is going somewhere and one of us needs to move, I'll come to Los Angeles. I'm just declaring that right now."

Because even though she loved Walker Beach, her future didn't have to be here to be beautiful. In fact, there was beauty in being comfortable enough with who she was to spread her wings and explore the world beyond the boundaries she'd set for herself.

"You'd do that?" Voice ragged, he cleared his throat.

"Yes." She angled her chin upward so he could see her eyes. See how serious she was. "I'm all in with you."

"Thank you, Shannon." He stroked her hair. "I don't know where the road will take us, but I'm all in with you too."

And, just as the prince would in any good fairytale, he sealed his declaration with a kiss.

EPILOGUE

*T*he fact that everyone else's life kept moving forward revealed how very stuck Jenna Wakefield's was.

Huffing out a breath, Jenna pulled a pair of dusty heels from deep inside Shannon's closet. She turned and dangled them from her fingertips. "I think you might need some new shoes."

Shannon looked up from the suitcase she was stuffing full of jean shorts and tank tops. "What? Why? There's nothing wrong with them. They still fit."

"Oh, girl." Jenna wrinkled her nose at the black monstrosities with wide, one-inch heels. "These are ugly old-lady shoes. And I'm sorry, my friend. I like you too much to let you wear these in New York. You will be laughed out of the state."

"She's right." Nose wrinkled in disgust, Gabrielle waddled into the room after her millionth trip to the bathroom. "I'm far from the fashion police, but even I say that those things have got to go."

As Gabrielle took a seat on the edge of the bed, one of her hands gripped her stomach, and she grimaced. Jenna noted the pallor in her sister's cheeks. She didn't remember ever looking that ghostly during her pregnancy with Liam. Then again, she'd been seventeen when she'd had him, so who knew what was considered normal.

Maybe Gabrielle had simply overdone it today. Apparently, Baby Girl had kept her up most of the night, and then after babysitting Liam this morning while Jenna went grocery shopping, Gabrielle had come over to Shannon's for lunch and packing.

Jenna touched her sister's shoulder. "Are you all right?"

Gabrielle waved her hand. "Oh, yeah. Just some Braxton Hicks. I think."

"Maybe you should call your doctor." Shannon looked as concerned as Jenna felt. "You didn't have to come over today. The weekends are your time to rest. You're already tired enough working full time."

Gabrielle was the mentorship program director at Tyler's charity foundation, Amazing Kids. She and Tyler had already made a trip to and from New York this month, but after how tired she'd been when they'd returned, Tyler had declared no more trips until after the baby came.

"I wanted the scoop on you and Marshall. Of course, I heard from several sources about the scene two days ago at the Frosted Cake, but I needed firsthand details."

"Which I happily provided." Shannon's cheeks still glowed, maybe partly from embarrassment, partly from ... well, love.

Jenna held in a sigh. What would it be like to have a purpose beyond surviving life as a single mom? To look forward to doing something she was passionate about?

To be in love with someone who loved her back?

Nope, nope, nope. Not going there, especially because she had a lot to be grateful for—her son, her sister, her brother-in-law, her soon-to-arrive niece.

Still, maybe someday she'd find a way to make a better life for Liam. He deserved it, even if she didn't.

"We're both super happy for you, Shannon." Jenna dropped

the heels onto the comforter beside a toiletries kit. "Now, to solve your shoe problem."

Breezing out the door, Jenna crossed the living room. Even though Shannon's sense of style was different than Jenna's—she tended toward brighter and bolder, while Shannon was all softness and pastels—they definitely shared a mutual love of art and interior design.

Jenna entered the guest room, where Quinn was staying for now. Though Shannon had forgiven her sister, Jenna remained skeptical of Quinn's intentions. One thing was for sure—Jenna would be watching out for Shannon and her far-too-sweet heart while Quinn was in town.

For now, there was at least one way the older sister could repay the younger for all the heartache she'd caused. And since Quinn wasn't here right now, Jenna would just have to help her make amends.

She dug around in Quinn's closet for a moment, found what she'd come for, and headed back to Shannon's bedroom.

"Here." She exchanged Shannon's heels with Quinn's sparkling silver Jimmy Choos. "These will go perfect with that little black dress you have shoved in the back of your closet."

"Are those Quinn's?" Her friend's eyes widened. Shannon shook her head. "I can't wear her shoes."

"Yes, you can. She more than owes you and you wear the same size." With Shannon's heels in hand, she turned.

"Where are you going with those?"

"Putting them in the trash where they belong. Believe me, I'm doing you a favor."

Ignoring Shannon's squeak of protest, she walked to the kitchen and dumped the shoes in their rightful place. Then Jenna made her way back to the bedroom, where Shannon held the Jimmys, stroking her fingers down the four-inch spikes. She glanced up. "I probably won't need heels anyway. I'll only be there for ten days, and I'm mostly going to help Marshall pack up his place."

Sounded like an adventure to Jenna. When was the last time she'd looked as happy as Shannon? Or gone anywhere exciting? Or...

Stop.

"Surely you'll have time for at least some touristy stuff," Gabrielle said. "There are so many iconic spots to see in the city."

"Many of which are perfect for kissing." Jenna wagged her eyebrows. "And also for declaring one's love to one's girlfriend."

"We've only officially been together for forty-eight hours." But her soft smile was a sure sign Shannon would return the sentiment if Marshall were to express it.

Which he totally would. Anyone who had seen them together knew Marshall St. John and Shannon Baker just fit. It wouldn't surprise Jenna at all if they were engaged by Christmas.

"She's right, Shan. That man is in love with you. He looks at you like Tyler looks at me." Gabrielle leaned forward as if to help Shannon as she resumed shirt folding, but groaned. "I'm sorry, ladies. I think I should get home and lie down."

"Of course." Shannon helped her ease off the bed into a standing position. "Should we call Tyler to come to get you?"

"I'll drive her." Jenna checked the clock on Shannon's side table. "I need to get home anyway. Cam is watching Liam for me, but I don't want to take up too much of his Saturday."

Exchanging a glance, Gabrielle and Shannon both smiled before her sister spoke. "I'm guessing he doesn't mind too much."

Jenna rolled her eyes, an automatic response when anyone teased her about her friendship with her boss. He was almost a decade older than her and tended to date women who were much more sophisticated than a former teen mom on antidepressants.

Even if she *had* dreamed of the day he might see her differently, it was never going to happen.

She helped Gabrielle to her feet. "Let's get out of here."

After dropping her sister off at home, Jenna headed to her own apartment complex. She checked her mail on the way in, flipping through the stack of bills as she walked toward her unit. Jenna spotted a rose-colored envelope. Stopping in the middle of the sidewalk, she examined it. Her name and address were scrawled across the front in fancy calligraphy, but there was no return address. Huh.

Jenna ran her finger under the lip of the envelope. From inside, she pulled out an invitation of some sort on heavyweight cardstock with gorgeous gold lettering.

You are invited to the inaugural meeting
of the Barefoot Sisterhood.
July 31st at seven p.m.
Barefoot B&B
Walker Beach, California
Dress is casual.
Bring yourself, your dreams ... and your discretion.

What in the world? Jenna flipped the mysterious invitation over for any clues about who had sent it, but there was nothing more.

Wait, the Barefoot B&B? Someone had purchased the old place next door to the Iridescent Inn over a month ago, but nobody in town seemed to know the identity of the new owner. And according to Carlotta Jenkins, public records showed some elusive corporation as the new owner.

And what was this about a sisterhood? Why would Jenna of

all people be invited? She wasn't anyone important. Maybe every woman in town had received an invite.

But still … it could provide a bit of fun. Excitement. Dare she say, adventure?

Goodness knew Jenna Wakefield could use a little more of each one in her life.

She tucked the invitation into her purse, pulled out her phone, and added the date to her calendar.

I hope you enjoyed Shannon and Marshall's story! I had so much fun writing it. In fact, I had so much fun writing the entire Walker Beach Romance series that I didn't want to stop. I love this town, with its quirks and its charm, and there are some more characters that I think deserve their own stories and happily ever afters—don't you? So come along with me and check out the first book of the Barefoot Sisterhood series, *The Inn at Walker Beach*.

CONNECT WITH LINDSAY

If you enjoyed *All You Need Is Love* (or any of my books, for that matter!), would you mind doing me a favor and leaving a review on Goodreads, Bookbub, or your favorite retail site?

I'd love to connect with you. Sign up for my newsletter at www.lindsayharrel.com/subscribe and I'll send you a FREE story as a thank you!

BOOKS BY LINDSAY HARREL

The Barefoot Sisterhood Series

The Inn at Walker Beach

Walker Beach Romance Series

All At Once (prequel novella)

All of You, Always

All Because of You

All I've Waited For

All You Need Is Love

Port Willis Series

The Secrets of Paper and Ink

Like a Winter Snow

Like a Christmas Dream

Standalones

The Joy of Falling

The Heart Between Us

One More Song to Sing

ABOUT THE AUTHOR

Lindsay Harrel is a lifelong book nerd who lives in Arizona with her young family and two golden retrievers in serious need of training. When she's not writing or chasing after her children, Lindsay enjoys making a fool of herself at Zumba, curling up with anything by Jane Austen, and savoring sour candy one piece at a time. Visit her at www.lindsayharrel.com.

facebook.com/lindsayharrel
instagram.com/lindsayharrelauthor

Walker Beach Romance Series

Book 4: All You Need Is Love

Published by Blue Aster Press

Cover: Hillary Manton Lodge Design

Editing: Barbara Curtis

CPSIA information can be obtained
at www.ICGtesting.com
Printed in the USA
BVHW031939060521
606690BV00014B/187